The Elusive Fox

Middle East Literature in Translation
Michael Beard and Adnan Haydar, *Series Editors*

Other titles from Middle East Literature in Translation

THE

Elusive Fox

MUHAMMAD ZAFZAF

Translated from the Arabic by
Mbarek Sryfi and Roger Allen

SYRACUSE UNIVERSITY PRESS

Syracuse University Press
Syracuse, New York 13244-5290

All Rights Reserved

First Edition 2016

16 17 18 19 20 21   6 5 4 3 2 1

Originally published in Arabic as *Al-ṭha'lab alladhī yaẓhar wa-yakhtafī*
(Casa: Manshūrāt Awrāq, 1989).

∞ The paper used in this publication meets the minimum requirements
of the American National Standard for Information Sciences—Permanence of Paper
for Printed Library Materials, ANSI Z39.48-1992.

For a listing of books published and distributed by Syracuse University Press,
visit www.SyracuseUniversityPress.syr.edu.

ISBN: 978-0-8156-1077-9 (paperback)   978-0-8156-5381-3 (e-book)

Library of Congress Cataloging-in-Publication Data
Names: Zafzāf, Muḥammad author. | Sryfi, Mbarek, translator. |
Allen, Roger translator.
Title: The elusive fox / Muhammad Zafzāf; translated from the Arabic
by Mbarek Sryfi and Roger Allen.
Other titles: Tha'lab alladhī yaẓharu wa-yakhtafī. English
Description: First edition. | Syracuse : Syracuse University Press, 2016. |
Series: Middle East literature in translation
Identifiers: LCCN 2016020131 (print) | LCCN 2016021912 (ebook) |
ISBN 9780815610779 (pbk. : alk. paper) | ISBN 9780815653813 (e-book)
Classification: LCC PJ7876.I4 T4313 2016 (print) | LCC PJ7876.I4 (ebook) |
DDC 892.7/36—dc23
LC record available at https://lccn.loc.gov/2016020131

Manufactured in the United States of America

The Elusive Fox

1

IN THE NAME OF GOD, the Merciful, the Compassionate, I will now begin by telling you the following story:

The city of Essaouira is like a woman, a woman both lock and key. I walked along its narrow alleyways, cautious and confused. Sometimes they were just wide enough for two people; at others they ended in a cul-de-sac. I checked in to the first hotel I saw and took a nap for about an hour; I had not had enough sleep the night before. A bit earlier I had been surprised by the weird behavior of a tomboyish girl; she looked like a young man but had a girl's voice. As I was standing in front of the hotel clerk, she took a quick look at me.

"Let him share my room," she said. "I've an extra bed."

"That's not allowed."

"So why do you let hippies do it then?"

"You're a Muslim woman. All the boss cares about is money. Go ahead and sleep with anyone you like, but the police poke their noses into everything."

"I'll be coming to your room during the night," the girl said. "Give him a room next to mine."

"You're trying to get me into trouble with the boss," the clerk said. "I'll throw your clothes outside."

"You think you can do that, do you? I'm a Zemouria, in case you've forgotten."

The clerk fell silent and handed me the key. She walked me upstairs, and another clerk followed us. She looked around the room.

"Do you want to kill him?" she said. "There's no glass in the window."

"Tell the boss when he comes in the evening," the clerk replied. "There are lots of hotels in Essaouira. Did we drag him here in chains?"

The clerk went away. She sat down beside me on the bed and took out a pack of cigarettes from between her breasts. Handing me one, she left.

I slept for about an hour. When I woke up, I was feeling nicely relaxed. Everything was calm and quiet—silent as the grave, no car engines, no human voices, completely calm. A light breeze was blowing through the broken glass. When I stood up and looked out the window, all you could see was a small yard with piles of trash and other stuff. There were closed windows as well, and the ones that were open had curtains. So nothing. Trash and windows closed, maybe closed on women. Before I came to visit the city, people told me that they—I mean women—may hide behind walls and clothes, but that in bed they do the kind of things that not even the devil's own wife would do. Living such a double life is wonderful; in fact, human life in general is full of ambiguity. People who choose not live that way have to be stupid. An endless tragedy. Why don't I say "comedy" instead? Human nature is both tragedy and comedy, so by definition it is ambiguous.

I could smell the fresh air coming in from the sea. The low buildings did not block my view. Outside the window the sky looked blue, clean and expansive, a welcoming sky that invites us to dissolve and hover like those tiny white clouds. So once again it is a case of everything or nothing. Sky, trash, and closed windows.

I left the window and put my head under the tap; the water was cool and refreshing. While I was drying my hair, I took out some of the money that I had put in the bag. Loosening my belt, I hid a few bills in the swimsuit pocket and put the rest in my pants.

It's hunger! I hadn't eaten since yesterday. When the bus stopped several times at the rest areas and passengers got off to buy meat and bread, I didn't dare do the same. I was afraid it would be old ewe's meat, which would give me diarrhea for two or three days. That had often happened to me before, and to other people as well. I closed the door and went downstairs. There she was, sitting in front of the clerk with her head between her hands. When she saw me, she leapt to her feet.

"Did you have a good sleep?"

As the clerk took the key from me, he kept looking at her out of the corner of his eye.

"Yes, I did sleep well," I said. "It was totally quiet. I had some dreams too, but I don't remember them."

"Me, too," she said. "I dream a lot in this hotel. It doesn't happen to me very often."

"Which city are you from?"

"I'm a gym teacher at a high school in Casablanca. What about you? You look like an artist. Do you paint? Act?"

"Neither. I'm a teacher."

"Strange. You don't look like one. Why do you keep your hair so long?"

"Oh, my hair! That's another story. A lot of people keep their hair long. That's not important. Do you know a place where I can get something to eat? I'm starving. I haven't eaten anything since yesterday."

"You look as if you don't eat well. You're skinny. Food's important for the body. You must eat, especially if you're smoking hashish. Do you smoke hashish?"

"Yes, sometimes, but I'm not hooked."

"Then you need to eat well."

A few people were sitting in the hall. A man in a djellaba had chosen to sit on one of the stairs. He had hiked his djellaba up to his knees, which showed his hairy legs; his homemade pants ballooned between his thighs. He was staring vacantly all around him, from chairs to people and up to the ceiling; it was as though this were the first time he had ever been in a hotel. As we left the hotel, the girl gave the clerk a defiant look, but he paid no attention.

"What do you want to eat?" she asked. "There are lots of restaurants. Grilled sardines, sandwiches?"

"I want a plate of tripe or cow's trotters."

"Sure. There are lots of popular restaurants as well, but they're a bit far."

We made our way through a number of narrow alleys where male and female hippies were sightseeing. Some of them were sitting on the ground or by a curb, while others were standing in front of the small shops, eating sandwiches (although I have no idea what was in them).

"My name's Fatima," the girl said, "Fatima Hajjouj. What do you think of the name?"

"It's wonderful."

"But it's just a plain old name, not like the names in TV movies and soap operas. What's your name?"

"Ali, but I don't think the rest is important."

"True enough, it doesn't matter. Names don't have to be important, but they can distinguish, for example, between different kinds of potatoes, tomatoes, or melons. People are just like potatoes, tomatoes, and melons: we need to give them names to distinguish them from each other. Still, never mind! Here we are. These restaurants all specialize in tripe, cow and sheep trotters, and steamed heads cooked the Essaouira way. They also have their own special way of preparing tagines that are different from ours."

It was about six in the evening. The sun was sinking in the west, but it was still bright. People did not look completely exhausted by their daily routines. The restaurants were operating alongside each other; not exactly restaurants, but big doors that opened on to three walls and a ceiling. We did the rounds first and then made our way into alleys that twisted and turned like a labyrinth. There were little apertures in the walls that revealed human beings, tagines, bread, and camel-meat kofta.

"I know these places well," Fatima said, "They're dirty, and they cheat you. Once I got a stomachache and had to stay in bed for a whole week; I couldn't stop vomiting, and both top and bottom. Could be you have no idea about this type of food."

Even so, people were wolfing it down, hippies as well, using fingernails, noses, cheeks, and hair.

"Just look at the way those people are eating," I said. "They couldn't care less about what you're saying."

"They're immune," she replied. "I'm not like them. If you want to eat, go ahead. No one's stopping you. I just wanted to let you see some food that won't make you ill."

With that she stopped in front of another restaurant where three peasants were sitting: one was sitting in a corner eating something, his face to the wall; the other two were seated on a mat, eating from the same plate. After looking at the plate on display by the dust-covered door, she went inside.

"The owner's a professional," she said. "He's good. Don't worry about his food. He's very clean and always washes his hands."

We sat down on the mat. Two of the peasants eyed us warily, then went back to their food. One of them was eating by stuffing all the fingers of his right hand into his mouth; when he took them out, they made a disgusting noise.

"One plate or two?" the owner asked.

"One well done," said Fatima.

"Make yourself at home," he said. "You know it all. You haven't brought any hippies here for quite a while. Are you angry with me or what?"

"No, I'm not," Fatima replied. "Either they prefer eating other stuff, or they don't have the money. As you well know, they spend a few days here, then leave."

"I know. But some of them come back once or twice a year."

The mat's color had faded, and parts of it were threadbare. Cutlery was by the door, and next to it was a box with all sorts of stuff piled in it. Alongside it was something that looked like a coat or blanket, apparently the place where the chef slept—if not him, then someone else. When I went to wash my hands, everything was filthy. I poured out some water, then dried my hands on my pants. The towel had obviously not been washed for days; it stank, and the stains were all sorts of different colors—from black to yellow and other colors with no names.

The chef spread out a sheet of newspaper and put a plate down in front of Fatima.

"Bon appétit!" he said, wiping his hands on an apron around his waist. "It's veal."

I devoured the entire plateful. Fatima had just a small piece. She kept smoking and flicking the ashes off by the

7

plate with the food I was eating and piling the butts on the newspaper. Once we had finished eating, she crumpled up the newspaper with the butts inside and put it all on the plate.

"Why don't you visit us more often?" the chef asked her. "Come even if you don't have any money. We're Muslims and should help each other."

"God willing," replied Fatima. "I don't like eating trotters all the time."

"Then you can't be hungry!" the owner replied with a laugh. "Porters have been coming here for years. They've had this meal for lunch and dinner. Just take a look at them, they're as strong as mules. If you came here, you'd never have to see the doctor. They all eat here and smoke hashish a lot, but they're still strong. Only one thing threatens them—tuberculosis. It's kif that causes that. I smoke too, but they smoke too much."

I handed him an American cigarette. He grabbed it eagerly and put it behind his ear. I gave him the money for the food, and we left. As we walked across a wide square, people were standing in front of piles of wheat, barley, grains, corn, and other vegetables. Some of them were shopping, while others were just enjoying the sunset and taking in the last rays of sunshine. Still others had already covered up their wares and had fallen asleep alongside them. People were heading in all directions, but only a few were buying anything.

"Morocco's doing well," Fatima said, pointing to the piles of grain. "Crops everywhere, and a meal costs just a dirham. Not so?"

"Definitely."

"No one's dying of hunger. Smuggled cigarettes and hashish are available everywhere."

"Absolutely."

"Life is beautiful."

"Yes, I know."

"Why do you always say 'yes'?"

"Because you're right."

"Okay. I thought you were making fun of me."

"I wouldn't do that. It's not in my nature to make fun of people. Life is beautiful, even if we had to eat on a threadbare mat a short while ago."

"What are you saying?"

"Nothing."

We crossed the square and went through an arch leading to the sea. I noticed women perched on a wall like storks or walking in every direction. There were very few men around. Maybe this is the way the city welcomes the evening: women near the sea and men in designated places.

As we strolled toward the sea amid this crowd of people, I felt Fatima put her arm in mine and surrendered myself to her gesture. For sure, other people in this crowd are behaving exactly the same way. So everything is possible.

2

AFTER ORDERING A CUP OF BLACK TEA, I sat down with a group of hippies on a bench. Some of them preferred to sit on the floor, while others lolled on the mat by the wall. Doors opened out on the café's courtyard. The rooms had previously served as court offices before the building was converted into a restaurant and hotel. Some other hippies, both men and women, were looking down from the first-floor balcony. Pop music could be heard . . . it was very loud.

"Do you mind?" asked the girl next to me.

"Go ahead."

I told her that, even though I didn't know what she wanted. I simply agreed. This place is a world I don't know; maybe it is different from Tangier and Marrakesh. The girl had shells in her hair and a snakeskin bracelet on her arm. She seemed totally at ease as she reached over to my cup of tea and took a sip. I had already noticed that people do that kind of thing around here even without asking permission. We took turns sipping tea. I handed the cup to another girl who was sitting on the floor a few feet away, but she declined.

"What I need's a tonic," she said.

She put the cup back on the table and pushed it towards me. "Are you a tourist," she asked, "or do you live here?"

"I only got here yesterday."

"The South's beautiful," she said. "We've visited Taroudant and Tantan; they're both beautiful. Everything there's authentic. We really liked going to the markets."

The music was still blaring. Men and women kept entering and leaving, some with shoes, others barefoot. A tall young man with long hair down to his shoulders and a Cyrano-type nose came over and stood right in front of us. The girl made some space for him next to her.

"This is Maxim, my fiancé," she said.

He did not pay us much attention but went ahead and ordered a 7-Up. Sweat was pouring off him. The man sitting next to him handed him a pipe full of kif. Cupping his hands, he started smoking and stared at the ceiling. He handed the pipe back to the same man, and he suggested that he pass it over to his fiancée. She took it from him, but, instead of taking a puff for herself, she handed it to me. I cupped my hand and did what Maxim had done. The pipe was made out of goat horn, with two strings attached, one red, the other green. I could feel the hashish I'd smoked making its way to my lungs. Handing the pipe back to the girl, I drank a sip of the tea, which was cold by now. It was black mint tea, and the mint leaves had settled in the bottom, filling almost half the cup. She handed the pipe back to her fiancé. "I don't like smoking," she said, looking at me. "I've tried, but I didn't like it."

"Trying's the basic issue here. It's addictive."

"What are you saying?" she asked. "I don't follow you. Listen to him, Maxim. He is saying things I don't understand."

Maxim handed the pipe to the other man and looked at us.

"What are you two saying?" he asked.

"I don't understand him."

"I told her that addiction's bad," I said. "Once you're addicted to something, you become a prisoner—meaning that you can't get rid of it. Things like patriotism, sex, and smoking."

Maxim stared at us in bewilderment. Because of the effect the kif was having, he had nothing to say, but even so he was listening to me.

"I don't understand what he's talking about," the girl went on. "The way he's talking sounds like philosophy."

"Let him talk," Maxim said. "Weird and wonderful things that lots of people never talk about. Ah yes, keep talking about habits. We all get used to doing things. What you're saying is true; maybe we've even got used to the way you talk. Isn't that so . . . ? What's your name again? Oh yes, Ali. Here you're all called Ali. I'm a newspaper photographer. What's your job?"

"Teacher."

"That's a great job. Does it pay well?"

"Not really."

"That's a shame!" he said, "Teachers and professors should be well looked after. I know of French professors who have the same issues as you're describing. Thank God I didn't become a teacher like you. She's is a teacher too. Her father's a grocer; he's from the Pyrenees."

"Excuse me," I told Maxim, "I need another cup of tea."

I gestured to the waiter, but he did not come for a while. A barefoot girl came over. She was wearing nasty, cheap Moroccan garb, but even so her legs looked clean and plump in the bright sunlight.

The young man did a double take.

"You can sit down," she told him.

"Thanks."

With that they both sat on the floor. He started looking for something inside his bag. At this point, I spotted Fatima coming in. That reminded me of "They ripped their girl's pocket. Oblivious to the sanctity of womanhood."

Her breasts were almost hidden and her chest was semi-flat—a man, a she-man, her gaze roaming everywhere. Once she had spotted me, she came over and squeezed in beside me.

"So here you are."

"Yep!"

"I've been looking for you for ages. I asked for you at the hotel."

"Hotels are just for sleeping," I said, "It's wonderful to discover other worlds. This is Maxim, and this is Brigitte."

Maxim begun to scrutinize her with his heavy, hashish-laden gaze. He took another pipe, thrust it under his long nose, then immediately handed it to Fatima.

"Great hashish!" she said.

She did not act shocked; actually, she was not of this world . . . I had the feeling that she had no sense of the world around her. She stood up and went over to say hello to a long-haired man with a ponytail tied back with a bright yellow rubber band.

"He's Italian," she said when she came back. "Poor guy! He was robbed. He'd like to continue his trip into the great African unknown. He says he has no money, but he's determined to continue with his journey."

"He's a liar."

"Don't say that. They're all that way. They don't have a penny, but they still travel. I don't know how they do it. A month or two later, they're sending you postcards from somewhere else in the world."

"I know, but not from the African jungle."

"Oh, that's something else."

The muscled waiter was wrestling with a thin young man and cursing him in English. The elephant and the ant, the fly and the bull—except that this time the fly could not defeat the bull. Four or five people crowded around them while everyone else stayed where they were, watching the action. Someone else paid the amount that the ant owed for the drinks he had had.

"He always does that," the elephant trumpeted in Arabic, addressing the aged owner. "He splits just as soon as he's finished drinking. Let me give him a good thrashing. I know these hippie types all too well!"

The old man gave a hand gesture and muttered something calmly . . .

"I heard this old man used to be a spice dealer," Fatima said, "and then he got rich in Essaouira. That all happened when he'd converted this place into a hotel and café."

"He's at death's door."

"Even so, he has no compassion. They say he's married to a sixteen-year-old girl. They brought her for him from Chichaoua."

"Why am I not surprised?!"

"I wish I were his wife. I'd know how to crush his balls for him . . ."

"You're a teacher. Such idle illusions are hardly appropriate!"

"We've all turned into illusions," she said, gesturing angrily. "You're one, and so is this person and that one and so on . . ."

"What's she saying?" asked Maxim.

"That we're all illusions," I told him in French.

"She's right!" he replied.

One is as crazy as another, I told myself. The young man at the bar was still shaking because he was afraid of the elephant. The music blared on, and customers kept arriving and leaving, some with shoes, others without.

3

THAT NIGHT I imagined the world as a graveyard in motion. Passersby on the narrow street looked like worms crawling their way over a gigantic, putrid corpse—the earth. They were all talking, frowning, and laughing, and, needless to say, hatching schemes against each other.

Somewhere else on this earth, in another street, some men are certainly busy killing each other, while others are blackmailing the weak, either by force or trickery. It's a game that is repeated throughout the ages, now adopting a serious guise.

How hard it is to talk in the first person; it's so scary for not only the self but also readers who keep searching in any number of books throughout their lives for something or other. But they never find it. After spending time procreating, they all land up in the grave. So it's back to the start . . .

Fatima stood there chatting to Maxim and his girlfriend, who were both seated about four spaces away from me.

"What are you thinking about?" she asked me. "Why don't you join us?"

"I was thinking about lots of things."

"Let's all talk about them," she suggested. "Maybe they're problems we could solve together."

"They aren't the kind of social things we can solve that way."

"I don't understand," she replied, "but never mind! They're suggesting that we get a couple of bottles of wine and go with them to their hotel room. I've suggested that we buy some grilled sardines first."

"As you like," I said. "Maxim seems to be clever."

"Definitely."

We made our way down the teeming narrow alleys. There were lots of local women wrapped up in white; only their pale arms and kohled eyes were visible. Other women were wearing European clothes, but they were mostly teenagers and students.

Fatima told me that she knew a Jew in town who sold wine. Alcohol could only be sold in three bars and the hotel; other liquor stores had either been closed by the local authorities or had their alcohol licenses revoked.

"All those women in wraps are whores," she added. "Essouira women are just like the ones in Khenifra."

"What's that you're saying?"

"You can hear!"

"I'm not hearing anything," I replied. "Don't say that to Maxim, or else he'll laugh at us."

"Why shouldn't I tell him?" she asked. "A woman who dances never covers her face."

In the end she did not tell him. Instead she kept kicking pebbles down the street.

We found ourselves in front of a small store, its brown door part of the newly whitewashed wall. "From this place?" she yelled at them both.

"Go in by yourself," she told Maxim. "He doesn't sell to Muslims. If he sees us together, he won't sell you the wine. He only sells to foreigners and policemen."

"What a weird country!" Maxim replied. "I don't understand a thing. I've seen Muslims drinking in bars. What's the difference between a bar and a grocery store?"

"Oh, dear," she said, "if you want to drink, then don't try to understand!"

"It's just a question," he said. "I'm not talking about politics. I realize you're not allowed to talk about that. I'm simply talking about normal things like eating, drinking, and sleeping. You mean, we can't even talk about them either!"

"In this country," said Fatima, "you're obliged to eat, drink, and shut up . . . and I mean drink water, not wine."

"But people drink wine."

"You don't understand," she said. "For Muslims alcohol is forbidden."

"But you all drink!" Maxim said. "In every Moroccan city, I've seen that with my own eyes."

"I'll explain it all to you later."

"Buy three or four bottles," I said as I lit a cigarette. "Later on you'll understand."

"Hashish is forbidden in our country too," Maxim said, "and yet you can smoke it freely in alleys, streets, and cafés. So what's the difference? Hashish is more dangerous than alcohol."

"You'll understand." I said. "I feel like a drink. You can go and talk to the Jew now."

"I'll go and talk to the Jew," Maxim said. "I realize that Jews get involved in everything, even the snow at the North Pole. I come from a Jewish family that converted to Christianity a century ago."

With that Maxim disappeared inside the dark store.

"He loves drinking," Brigitte said, "but he hasn't drunk a lot in Morocco. You should see the way he drinks back there."

"In France, you mean?"

"Yes. He loves Bordeaux wine. He's just like my father, although my father drinks too much. He drinks fast so he can get drunk as quickly as possible."

By the port there were rows of meat grills. Long benches had been set up close by, and Moroccans and foreign hippies were sitting there, speaking a host of different languages and devouring hot sardines savored with squeezed lime juice. Other people preferred sitting on the ground near a lake that reeked of sardines; all around you could hear flies buzzing. Maxim trailed behind us, carrying a plastic bag. He looked distracted but showed no signs of being tired or anything else.

"People prefer eating sardines hot," Fatima told me, "straight from the fire to their guts—from sea to fire to stomach. By the time they get cold, they've lost a lot of their flavor."

"Let's eat a bit," Brigitte suggested, "and then we can take the rest of it with us."

"Good idea!"

The two girls decided the whole thing. All we two men had to do was go along with the plan. Nets were spread out on the sidewalk a few meters away—fishing boats, sea, island, horizon, then another world beyond that horizon, America. Perhaps on the opposite east coast shore in America there were also people at the same time, eating sardines and thinking about us, telling themselves that the world is small and the only thing dividing us is a waterway.

Fish glistened in the sunlight as they were emptied into boxes right in front of us, while other tempting seafood items like crabs, shrimp, and scallops were being carefully collected. People kept crowding around, some sitting, others standing, as they watched the fish being unloaded from the boats. They may also have been bartering; I don't know. Everywhere you could smell grilled sardines; everyone was devouring them with relish. The hippies did not like eating them with bread, something the grillers were well aware of. That is why the hunks of bread were given to the Moroccans.

We ate and took some sardines away with us. Fatima advised me not to eat hot chili, but, in spite of her advice, I did eat one. I'm still sweating.

"Didn't I tell you?" she asked, sensing my discomfort. "You're destroying your stomach and health."

"But it gives you an appetite."

"It's better to eat when you're hungry."

"Next time I'll do that."

"Are you joking?"

"No, I swear. With women like you there's no joking."

"What's the difference?"

"You know!"

"Are you two having a fight?" Maxim asked with a laugh.

"No. She's giving me a lecture on hot chili."

"Oh, great!" he said. "Women can give lectures on anything, even hot chili. That bitch behind us sometimes gives me lectures even though she's no good at talking. But when it's time for the lecture, her tongue cuts loose. The problem is that I'm not a good student or listener."

She was sitting close to him and heard him talking loudly about her. Even so she said nothing; it was not yet time for her lecture. The other woman stopped talking about the evils of hot chili. We walked down a whole series of narrow, labyrinthine alleys till we reached the Haven of Rest Hotel where Maxim and Brigitte were staying. The clerk was dozing behind the wooden screen, with the key rack behind him. He roused himself with a yawn.

"Not allowed," he told Maxim.

"What?"

He pointed at Fatima. "That woman can't go into a hotel room with males," he said.

"What are you saying, you pimp?" Fatima asked in Arabic.

The clerk looked startled. He probably was not expecting such a reaction, but he recovered his self-confidence.

"What you've just said isn't polite," he told her. "You seem to be from a decent family. I'm simply following the hotel owner's instructions."

Then he craned forward to look inside the plastic bag on the counter in front of him. "Let me have a bottle," he went on, "and I can pretend I didn't see anything."

"Good God!" Fatima said, "You won't get a single drop."

"What's going on?" Maxim asked.

"He's asking for a bottle."

"Simple enough, isn't it!"

The clerk smiled as Maxim took out a bottle and handed it to him. With the bottle clutched to his chest, the clerk turned his attention away and went back to his seat, as happy as a baby. There was no more protest, no following of owner's instructions, and no worries about the police. See no evil, hear no evil. We all went up to the room, and Brigitte closed the old red curtains. Maxim put the bottles on the small table next to an old chair and sink with a piece of mirror behind it on the wall.

"Okay, now we should relax," Maxim said. "Ali, give me a hand, and we'll put this mattress on the floor."

Fatima jumped up. "Let him be," she said. "I don't think he can lift it."

She grabbed the mattress by two corners, Maxim did the same on the opposite side, and I took the middle. With that we moved the mattress to the floor. Brigitte watched the whole thing in bewilderment; she seemed scared of something. The three of us sat cross-legged on the mattress, but Brigitte chose to sit on the chair. Fatima put the soggy grilled sardines on a newspaper on the floor, then handed Brigitte the only glass which was by the sink under the mirror.

"I only want one glass of wine," she said. "If Fatima has any hashish, I'd much prefer that."

"I've got a small piece, but it's enough to make an entire tribe high. Come and sit down here with us. Don't stay perched up there like a stork."

"I prefer the chair for now."

"As you wish!"

Maxim used his fingernails to open the bottle and poured himself a swig.

"It's good," he said, smacking his lips.

"It's only *vin ordinaire*."

"It's still good."

Fatima took out the piece of hashish wrapped in a piece of paper, opened it, and begun to burn the edges. After going through her entire ritual, she started smoking with Brigitte and Maxim. I preferred not to smoke.

"Why aren't you smoking?" Maxim asked.

"When I'm drinking, it doesn't agree with me. It can make me vomit or give me a bad headache."

"You know your own self better than anyone else."

But how do I know myself? Who among us really knows himself? Many a time I've kidded myself that I do. I'm well aware of certain habits and chronic urges that control my behavior. But such things quickly propagate and generate still more habits and urges. I'm always surprised that they are coming from me, as though from someone else.

"Know myself! That's a joke."

"What are you saying?" Maxim asked as he handed me the glass.

"Nothing. All I said was that I really know myself."

"It's wonderful for people to know themselves."

"Never do anything that'll cause you harm."

Brigitte stood up and went over to a bag in the corner to look for a radio. When she turned it on, first there was a hissing noise, then came the music. She turned it up, but Maxim asked her to turn it down again. She immediately did so.

"You're just like Mr. Seguin's goat in the story," he told her. "You always behave like a child. I've no idea what you do with your students in class."

She gave him a scared look, and her expression made it clear that she was upset. I noticed tears welling in her eyes.

"You're always being nasty to me, Maxim. What do I do to you?"

"You're just like a lump of dough. Be more like Fatima: smoke some hashish and shut up."

Putting the radio down on the table, she went over, gave him a kiss, and sat next to him. Maybe he felt a bit embarrassed, I don't know, but that's what I thought. Fatima was not paying any attention to what was going on around her; she was just enjoying the hashish. After handing the joint to Brigitte, she leaned her elbows on the mattress, stretched out her legs on the floor, and started staring at the ceiling while her body swayed to the rhythm of the music—which continued uninterrupted by any words from the announcer. "Fantastic music!" Brigitte said. "It must be the Gibraltar radio station."

"No," I responded. "It's either Spanish or else Rabat's international station. You can only pick up the Gibraltar station in northern Morocco."

"Oh, I see," said Brigitte, "I didn't know that. Do you get Radio France International here?"

"Shut up! You're just like Mr. Seguin's goat in the story," Maxim told her. "How many times have I told you you're just stupid?"

"But Maxim," she replied. "I just want to know, but you'll never let me find out. In my place you'd want to know."

"What are you saying?"

"Nothing, my love."

He looked at me. "Just listen to her!" he said.

"Let her say whatever she wants," I replied. "It's better to let people say what they want even if it's about politics and religious beliefs. Without that, we can never get at the truth."

"But we can't get there by spouting nonsense. Throughout history lots of people have done just that, but they haven't managed to staunch the wound."

"Never mind," I said. "That's another matter. Just pour me another glass and let Brigitte prattle on. Here we all are today, sitting in a dark room at midday. Truth is being lost right here in this room."

Fatima stood up, spread her arms like eagle's wings, and started dancing, seemingly floating in a clear sky. Just then she heard a soft knock on the door and reached for the knob. The hotel clerk's head appeared.

"Do you want some terrific hashish at a good price?" he asked.

"No, thanks," Fatima replied.

She handed him what was left of the joint.

He took it with a smile. "I just came to tell you I love you all," he told them. "I won't betray you. If you need some really good hashish, just let me know."

"No, no, thanks!" Fatima told him. "They don't smoke. It's only me."

The clerk closed the door and left. Fatima resumed her dance.

"What an ass!"

Maxim stood up barefoot and started dancing with Fatima. Meanwhile Brigitte started rolling another joint, the contents of which she had taken from a box on top of the mattress. There was still no announcer on the radio, and the music continued. When she poured me another glass, I could feel a change in my body, something like ants crawling around inside my brain. Wide vistas opened before me, as wide as the room itself, while Fatima kept floating across the space. The window opened up as well, and I could smell a nice breeze wafting through it. So this is glory in life at its fullest, an everyday glory.

Maxim was now close to Fatima. When the music changed, he clung to her as they started dancing like two lovers who had been kept apart for years. After a while, they sat down again on the mattress, without looking at all tired. Brigitte had lit the joint and taken a deep drag, all the while moving her head gently in time with the music. Maxim took the joint, took a drag, then handed it to Fatima. She tried to tempt me, but I refused. I emptied the glass in one gulp, then filled it up for Maxim.

"Thanks," he said.

The harsh gleam in his eyes reflected the color of the room. I heard him humming the words of an English song.

"Have you ever visited France?" he asked Fatima.

"No."

"But you speak French fluently."

"Of course. I studied it in school."

"I mean, you speak it like a French person, with no accent."

"I don't know."

"Ali has an accent," he said. "He speaks like the Occitan in France."

He looked over at Brigitte. "Get up, you bitch," he yelled, "and dance with Ali!"

She was still staring at the ceiling and ignored him. She was not wearing a bra, so when she unbuttoned her shirt, she showed part of her breasts. She was of medium build, neither fat nor skinny, just like Fatima, except that Fatima was taller, more masculine, and had short hair. Brigitte took the cigarette from her; before taking another deep puff, she mumbled something.

Getting slowly to her feet, she started weaving her way around the room quietly and softly. The hotel clerk came back to offer his product again, but this time Fatima declined politely. He kept smirking.

"That mule looks drunk," said Maxim.

"And high too!"

"Are we the only ones in the hotel?"

"No, that can't be right."

He smiled as he said that. When he pulled Fatima toward him, she leaned longingly into his chest. He started running his fingers through her short hair, and I watched as she closed her eyes. Brigitte meanwhile was doing her best to imitate a belly dancer, twisting her body in slow motion. Maxim now lay on his back with Fatima on top of him. I took the glass from him and filled it up for myself. Angrily I smoked two cigarettes, one after the other. Brigitte called me over, and I joined her in the belly dance. Moving her arms slowly in the air, she kept a space between us. Grabbing me by the hand, she twirled me round and then moved away to perform some peculiar moves in front of the wall. I went back to my spot to fill the glass from the other bottle while Maxim's hand kept searching for something on Fatima's body.

So then, this is today's everyday glory.

Getting to my feet, I turned on the light to counter the evening gloom. As I watched the goings-on inside the room, I enjoyed drinking the wine. Once in a while I would recall images from the past, but they would rapidly dissolve.

Brigitte tossed her shirt into a corner and continued her crazy routine, still gyrating slowly. Her eyes remained closed, and she was lifting her hands in the air with her fingers splayed. Eventually she came over and sat in my lap.

"Ali," she asked, "are you drunk?"

"Not yet."

"You don't seem to be."

She put her arms around my neck. Her breasts were touching my chest, and a strong heat emanated from her upper body. It's the eternal call.

4

FOR THREE DAYS, I have not had enough sleep. Around here everyone stays up late. You encounter people everywhere; they talk to you easily, spontaneously, and without fear. Some share a sandwich with you, others a soda or a cup of tea; still others invite you to travel with them to the North or South for free. These days lots of cars appear one day, only to vanish the next.

I used to love wandering around aimlessly, walking from one alley to the next. There were hippies everywhere, living mostly in cheap hotels or small dark rooms, in neighborhoods such as Ahl Agadir, the old Mellah, Bni Antar, Haddada, and Sandio. They all seemed just like mice, coming out of their holes to eat and then going back.

During those three days, I did not see Fatima; she seems to have been traveling somewhere else. I don't know. The only thing I do know is that, after that night, I went back to the hotel by myself early in the morning, drunk and exhausted, and stayed in bed until the evening. I tried to vomit but without success; all that happened was that I belched up the stench of cheap wine, sardines, and cigarettes. The thing that I was afraid might happen did. When I finally woke up, I did not want to eat anything. By now it was evening, and I don't like that because it reminds me of the end of the universe. Everything goes to bed so that the farce can continue—the great farce, that gigantic circus where all dispositions assemble and repeat themselves throughout the course of history: love, hatred, justice, tyranny, hypocrisy, theft, and good behavior, all wrapped in motives that at least initially may be genuine.

Now it's evening again. Everything has happened today, but I've been away. Actually, even when I'm fully awake, I'm almost always not present. How many things that happen get repeated one time or another. This is evening: for them it marks the end of things, but for me the beginning. But without them those same things can't be mine too; they make me feel that those things are mine as well. It's a nice, ancient game, part of the great farce, the comedy, the big circus. I've had to adopt a role in this circus; I don't know how to do the bear, lion, or tiger, but I can manage the donkey and mule very well. However, since humans despise both of them, I've preferred to be a fox tonight, especially since after a long day the flock is exhausted. When I was a child, I read a lot about wily foxes in school textbooks and heard a lot as well. The flocks of sheep kept walking along the narrow alleys in groups, while a few dawdling scabby ewes kept dragging their feet and sticking close to the walls; they were chewing over their daily worries and thinking about others to come and how they would go about solving them. Who knows, maybe death will surprise them and put an end to it all. For ewes, problems never end. No sooner is one solved than another one crops up. Even if you don't possess that almighty, invisible hand that plays its part in creating these problems, ewes can still manage to create them for themselves and others as well. Out of a sense of compassion for these ewes that have not learned any lessons from the dwindling and disappearance of previous flocks over years gone by, that same almighty, invisible power has created something called death, which is true wisdom, the eternal lesson that is still trying to teach every single ewe but in vain.

So now here they are, walking all around me. They have been grazing on someone else's daily grass without a single pang of regret. I have just remembered the words of the Arab poet Umar Ibn Abī Rabi'ah who said, "It is only the weak who do not oppress." Even so, tonight I have insisted on keeping my fox role, not a ewe. But no one has paid any attention to my snout or tail; at any moment I might pounce on one of them. But whether their heads are raised or lowered, they seem completely oblivious. They keep walking slowly along the alleys in groups, although a few of them seem to be in a hurry. They keep barging into each other with their shoulders and craning their necks to reach out to their fellows. It's evening!

I found myself in the Taghart neighborhood, with its wide open spaces, the expanse of the sea, and the island that looks like a rock in the middle of the sea. The streetlights in Taghart have been turned on, and from the deserted island comes a faint light, maybe drunkards or fishermen, or even a wolf that prefers to be isolated from the pack. Never mind! This too is something beautiful, the exception to the rule.

I walked towards the sea, went into the Chalet café and ordered a cold beer. The Chalet was a cage in the circus, where different species of animals come together for the time being but might well change their temperament at some point in the future. I sat by the edge of the counter, downing my beer with gusto. I don't need to describe everything inside this cage, but that doesn't prevent me from noting that the entire place was filled with a quiet chatter that managed to combine both fear and caution. That may well have been because the customers felt they had been caught out: the injunction "selling alcohol to Muslims is forbidden" dated from colonial times and was still very much on their minds. But, beyond all that, these particular animals preferred to get away from the flock, like the bear on the island. It was simply an impression they all had. Just as the sheep flock can envisage its own grass and that of others as well and work out how to get hold of it, so have I the right to envisage the bears on the island. They have all chosen a different way of life. That's even though I am a fox; I'm already well aware that the bear on the island has a better life than the flock of sheep. Bears and the various other animals in the Chalet café despise the very idea of eating ewes; that is simply good behavior. And why shouldn't such a thing happen for the very first time during this entire period when the strong have always oppressed the weak? Ewes are stupid and naïve; that's the way they have always been through the ages. So let's leave them to stay far away, making their way toward the barn. It won't be long before they fall asleep, ready to wake up again in order to go out and graze the next day and the day after that. That's not important. But I have to hide my tail, in case the animals inside this cage resume their original temperament and discover that I'm a fox. I'm not a fox; at this particular moment I'm simply an animal just like them. Whatever is going to happen can happen. End of story.

"Another beer, please."

"Excuse me?"

"A beer."

"Another cold beer?"

"Yes. A cold beer."

He said that without even glancing at the waiter. The beer was right in front of me, cold and inviting. I realize that carbonated drinks are bad for me, but never mind. Let me have a drink, and whatever happens will happen. I remembered a Spanish sailor in a Casablanca bar, downing one beer after the other and dipping bread in hot sauce. When he guessed that his behavior surprised me, he turned and looked straight at me. His face and jowls were bright red, and he was sweating profusely. "Are you surprised I'm eating it with such relish?" he asked with a smile.

"No, sir, I'm not," I replied. "I'm just absent-minded, that's all. I can stare either here or there; it makes no difference."

"Do you have problems?"

"Could be."

"Forget the problems and have a drink," he said. "The time you're living in, that's all you have. Let me tell you something. I'm a sailor and I own real estate, thanks be to God, Jesus, and the Virgin Mary! But that's not what I'm getting at. Over ten years ago, I contracted a disease; I've no idea what it is. I've been to see doctors, and they have all insisted that I need to quit using the substances I've been addicted to—coffee, smoking (I don't smoke), drinking beer, and eating hot chili. If I didn't stop, they all told me, I'd be dead in six months at the most. That's what they all said, and yet here I am, as you can see, still alive. If the Virgin Mary so wills, I'll live even longer. Doctors talk too much. They all advise you to quit drinking tea, coffee, beer, citrus fruits, cigarettes, and stew, and instead to take walks. Do you understand me?"

"Yes, sir," I replied. "That may be the case where you are, but exactly the same thing happens here too."

The image of the Spaniard and the bar in Casablanca disappeared. I gulped down the second beer and asked for a third. I kept turning around to check that tail of mine on the stool in front of the wooden counter. I must have done it several times because it was the café owner who spoke to me when he opened my third beer and not the waiter.

"You keep fidgeting on that stool. What's the matter with you? Do you have hemorrhoids or something? Don't even mention hemorrhoids, I have them too. Let me give you a piece of advice: I'll bring you some ice cubes. Take them with you to the bathroom and put them on your anus. You'll see the result for yourself."

"Actually I don't have hemorrhoids. It's my tail, my fox tail."

"What are you talking about? You aren't even drunk yet."

"No, I'm not. I'm just talking about my tail."

"I understand. That's fine, talking about hemorrhoids that way, calling them your tail. It's fine for people to feel bashful about it."

The owner went out, came back with some ice cubes, and thrust them into my hand.

"Go to the bathroom," he told me. "Don't be embarrassed. You should take care of your health. Go to the bathroom and do as I've told you."

I felt scared that my situation might be discovered—he might figure out that I'm a cunning fox, so I gave in to him. If he did find out, he might well be a lion himself. I went to the bathroom and threw the cubes in the toilet. After pissing and smoking a cigarette, I came back to my place.

"How do you feel now?" he asked me.

"The pain's going away."

"Didn't I tell you? Ask someone with experience, not doctors. Now you'll have a beer on me."

He put another beer in front of me. Outside it was nighttime, the master of all creatures who belong to half the Earth, while the sun is the master of the other half.

"Are you from Marrakesh?" asked one of the animals next to me.

"No. Casablanca."

"How come you're so dirty then?" he asked. "Get yourself a job and leave the hippies to themselves. Why are you behaving like them? Cut your hair and come work with us as a fisherman. Lots of youngsters from Essaouira have gone crazy, smoking hashish and getting stoned all day long. Be sensible. One day you'll get old, and there'll be no one to take care of you. You'll turn into a commodity, a disused piece of trash that's been tossed away by the roadside. Do you understand me?"

"Yes, I do," I replied. "Thanks! I'm going to follow your advice. The genuine Muslim is someone who can give advice to his fellow Muslims."

I watched as he looked at me, staring down at my feet and behind my back. I touched my face to make sure it did not have a fox's snout and ran my hand down behind the stool to make sure that my tail was still out of sight. When I had reassured myself that I looked just like everyone else, I tried to run for my life and leave the café.

"Get a beer," the animal said, "and let's chat for a bit."

"No, thanks, I've an appointment."

"God help you!"

Leaving the café, I made my way warily through the Taghart neighborhood. By now the ewes had all left, but some lambs were still frolicking around, apparently unaware that there was a fox in their midst. Who knows, maybe some of the other foxes are smarter and more dangerous. For my part, I know how to keep my own cunning out of sight. I reached the Café de France and sat at the counter. When the waiter came over, I ordered some cake because I could not drink any more after swigging all that beer. Next to the café there was a newspaper kiosk. I noticed some newspapers hanging there and thought about buying a few, but then I changed my mind.

"Ali!" I heard a voice just behind me. "What are you doing alone?"

It was a young unemployed man from Casablanca whom I had met at the Comedie café. The only thing I know about him is that he lives off his two prostitute sisters and occasionally foreign homosexuals. I had also run into him in Tangier, Marrakesh, and wherever else homosexuals were. I stood up immediately and went over to sit with him. He had four girls around him who kept nodding their heads nonchalantly. Only one of them gave me so much as a welcoming glance.

"Hello," she said. "Have a seat. You've got beautiful long hair. If you washed it, it would be even nicer."

I nodded.

"You're a lucky man!" said `Abduh in Arabic. He was sitting on a chair but kept shifting his entire body with long arms dangling. "That bitch hasn't said a single word to me. I only met them this morning."

"Why don't you have something to drink?" she suggested in poor French.

"I had a beer not long ago."

"Oh," she said, "I don't like alcohol. My father belongs to an anti-alcohol group in Sweden."

The square was almost devoid of Moroccans. Groups of hippies made their way across it, with and without shoes. In front of the café, there were some cars with a variety of foreign license plates; they were not luxurious or modern, but the rugged kind that can put up with any kind of road. I finished the cake and lit a cigarette. From inside the café, I could hear the TV blaring; there were some words in Egyptian dialect, but I could not make out a single sentence. It was obviously one of those Egyptian movies about love, the Prophet's biography, or famous figures in Islamic history, they being the favorite topics for Eastern Arabs or, at any rate, what is regularly shown on Rabat's TV channel.

`Abduh kept trying his best to attract the girls' attention, speaking in a Parisian French accent and occasionally in English as well. The girls kept smiling.

"You don't have much to say," the Swedish girl told him. "You look as though you're suffering somehow. You're so gloomy."

"You're right," I said. "I'm sad because I don't have any money. Somebody stole it." (That's what the fox told her, not me. If you happened to frisk me, you'd spit in my face.)

"This bitch isn't like the other ones I've met here," Ali said. "She's crazy and very pretty. Don't you think so?

She's fond of someone who lives in a shack near Dyabat who has been raving on and on to her about religious stuff."

"What's he doing in that shack?"

"It's just that he's illiterate. He begs in Jamaa Lafna in Marrakesh, then comes back to the shack and . . . manages to kid stupid women like this that he's a prophet. You should take her away from him. You deserve her more than he does."

"She's really cute. She looks a bit weird too."

"She's nuts! There are too many crazy people in Essaouira."

"They are not crazy. If they were, they would not have been touring the entire world without a single penny in their pockets. They're really smart. Their upbringing is different from ours."

"You may be right. You're a teacher, so you know more about those things."

As he talked, he kept fidgeting; once in a while, his long, thin arms would take over the communication.

"`Abduh," one of the girls asked, "are you going to come to Dyabat with us?"

"Sure. Every night there are parties in the open air."

"We know that."

"Have you ever visited Dyabat?" `Abduh asked me.

"No," I replied, "but I've heard about it."

"It's a fishing village. All the hippies live there; it's dirt-cheap. You can rent a shack and be as free as you want. It's better than the hotels here. I know how hotel owners operate, not to mention police harassment. In Dyabat, even the gendarmes get stoned so they can join us in making passes at the hippy girls. But the girls resent them. I have never seen a gendarme manage to land a single one of them."

A cart passed by carrying a folk band and bags of flour and sugar. The musicians were playing, while a man in woman's clothing was shaking his backside. A few people were clustered around the cart clapping, and a few children as well. Occasions like this usually attract lots of children, but at this time of night most parents prefer to keep their doors closed with children inside.

The waiter came over, and each of us paid for his drink. When we all stood up, she latched on to me. She was wearing a loose-fitting, colored dress; to me she looked like a gypsy or even something nonhuman—anything but, in fact. As long as the imagination can envisage things at will, it can muster any kind of being to represent her.

"Of course. You're going to come to Dyabat with us, right? Have you been there before?"

"No."

"It's a beautiful village. But I prefer another place near it called 'An-Nab.'" A man called Omar lives there. He has a close relationship with God and talks to him like Moses. Don't you think that's wonderful? He might be in Marrakesh now. Sometimes he's away for three or four days a week, and occasionally it's even longer. Do you know this young man with us?"

"Not much."

"I'm not happy with him."

"He is a poor, miserable young man."

"More than that, he looks like a liar."

"I've no idea."

"I'm just guessing. Come on, let's get in the car with the girls. I don't own a car even though I'm not poor."

We all squeezed into the back seat, and once again she nestled up to me. She felt warm and had a special scent to her. Her body felt fresh and inviting. The very idea made me shiver all over. All the barriers separating human beings collapsed. That eternal entity that haunts us while we're alive now called; we may try to escape it, but it haunts us nevertheless. I could not stop myself raising my arm and encircling her neck and hair. She surrendered and put her head on my shoulder. `Abduh was still fooling around. I had no idea what he was saying because I was dreaming of something else. As the car passed through the Taghart neighborhood on the road to Agadir, the girls' voices kept getting louder and blending with each other.

"My name's Salma." she told me in a low voice.

"Salma Lagerlöf."

"Oh, you know the name. She's the writer, the Nobel Prize winner. She's from my country. I had this hunch that you'd know everything; it didn't let me down. It can never be wrong. Have you read any of her work?"

"Yes."

"What have you read?"

"I can't remember any more."

"Have you read any other Swedish authors?"

"Yes, but I don't remember their names. I remember Salma because Arabs use the name."

"Right, that's true."

"Yes!"

The car turned on to a dirt road between overgrown trees. There were a lot of potholes, so the car was having a difficult time. Salma's head kept bumping my chin. She heard my teeth chattering and sat up straight. Even so, she still seemed fresh; beneath the thin dress she was wearing, her body still felt warm and soft. Her bodily warmth was being transferred to mine and getting warmer by the second. On either side of the road, the trees lined up in the car's headlights. Elena handed us a joint; I took a drag, then handed it to Salma. She took a deep puff, then gave it back to one of the girls. Soon after, we arrived at the Dyabat village beach. There was a series of small buildings huddled together in the dark. `Abduh jumped out and so did we. The sound of music echoed through the quiet night, and the sea waves glistened beyond the trees.

"Shall we go to the Danish girl's house," one of the girls asked, "or to those other folk? She always gives new people a warm welcome."

As she talked about "those other folk", she pointed to an isolated old building, a mansion a few meters from where we were standing; the music we could hear was coming from there. No one bothered to answer her question, but we simply started walking toward the mansion. I was at the back, and Salma was glued to my side. I did not realize that she was barefoot, but then her foot crashed against a stone and she yelled. We found ourselves facing a big gate. We made our way down some stone steps and walked in the dark along narrow streets. There were buildings on either side, but we could not tell whether they were houses or shops. No one was around. We got closer to the source of the music, and I started hearing human voices mixed with the sound of drums. Eventually we reached a square where a group of male and female hippies were gathered. It was circular in shape; in the middle was a fire burning wood and branches that managed to light up the whole place.

"Let's sit," Salma suggested. "Here's better. I don't like crowds."

I agreed without saying a word. She sat on the ground and so did I, while the other girls sat a bit further away from us, behind the circle of people clustered around the fire.

"No doubt, this is the way primitive people used to do things," I thought. "It's all assembled here now: water, air, fire, and the earth I'm sitting on."

Salma began nodding her head in time with the music. Her hair was flying all over the place and covered her face. But then she stopped and moved closer to me. I kept staring at the strange world all around me. Some people were asleep, while others were dancing and singing in a language I did not understand. Several couples were clutching each other without attracting anyone else's attention. Salma lay down on her back and put her head on my thigh. I did not like that and dearly wished that it could be the other way round. If we were behaving like everyone else, I would have been thrusting my hands between her breasts. She felt a particular sensation and turned over on the ground. Now I too stretched out on my back, and she moved until we were face to face. I gave her a hug, and we became entwined, two in one. However, a muscular man carrying a bucket stood right in front of us.

"You're from Casablanca, right?" he asked, handing me the bucket. "My name's Mustafa, and I'm from Marrakesh. Welcome. How did you manage to get this one?"

"Do you all know her?"

"Who does not know this little fool? She's beautiful, though. I wish she'd fall in love with me. She's not like the other girls. Help yourself, take some *ma'jun*, it helps in bed."

Salma put her hand in the bucket and grabbed some *ma'jun*.

"I love *ma'jun*," she said. "How about you?"

"Me too!"

I followed her lead. The man went over to another group. My tongue kept searching my mouth for the remains of the *ma'jun*. I adored its taste. I kept staring at the fire, the people all around me, and the shadows reflected on the walls with their fading whitewash. Everyone was sitting, but three people kept vaulting over people's heads. I had no idea what they were doing or saying. These were rituals I knew nothing about. Apart from the music, everything else was normal, except for the extraordinary beauty of some of the girls. As long as a beautiful female was by my side, I preferred lying on my back and staring up at the stars. Salma did the same thing. I sensed that she was still chewing on something.

"Tasty, isn't it?" I said.

"Great, awesome," Salma replied. "I love it. It is better than LSD. I don't like synthetic stuff. I like it natural. But then, I'm not a drug addict."

"I'm like you," I said. "But I like a drink occasionally."

"I have the impression," she commented, "that you could give up drugs, but not drinking."

"People can never give up drink," I replied. "It's like sex, air, water, and food."

"I didn't realize that," she said. "Didn't I say a while ago that you know a lot of stuff? Even so, I won't drink."

Rhythms always spread in space; once in a while there's a short break. Then the music starts again, and voices get louder. We paid no attention to all that. When I brushed Salma's eyelids with my fingers, she closed her eyes. For sure, she was not asleep. My eyelids felt heavy as well. The stars started to dance in the sky before my very eyes. When the darkness began to turn into iridescent colors, I decided to close my eyes and let my fingers do whatever they wanted with Salma's body. She was quiet and warm, desirable and wise, full and fresh, a dreamer and other things as well; the rest can come from your imagination. Later I opened my eyes to the first rays of sunlight. There were only about ten people left, stretched out on the ground, and ashes in the middle of the square. Every couple was a unit. Following their lead, I put my head underneath Salma's armpit so as avoid those first rays of sunshine . . .

5

A FEW DAYS LATER, I left the hotel and rented a house in the village for a much cheaper price. Whenever life becomes cheaper here, time gets extended. What do I have to do in Casablanca? There is no one in particular waiting for me there; just a dirty room, toilet, and shower; a sponge mattress to sleep on, a rug, and books piled all over the floor. What else? Three or four female teachers who love me a lot at the beginning of the month. They help me squander my miserable paycheck for the first few days. Oh, my God! How they love to drink, especially when it is free! But again I ask, what else is there to do in Casablanca? Spend the whole night with friends, going from one bar to the next. No night ever passes without fights involving hands, legs, and tongues. They are all trying to write, and the lucky few who get published are the ones who fall prey when everyone gets plastered.

It is the sixties, and I have no idea what things will be like in the seventies and eighties. Will new generations emerge just like this one? Will everything be repeated? I have often asked myself that question while standing in front of the students. What will become of those male and female hippies later in life? Let's leave the answer to the next two decades. One should always look to the future, but that is precisely what people habitually refuse to do, and that is the root cause of all their daily problems. Just look back at the past, and then contemplate the future. Indeed, let us do just that even though nothing is certain for us. By indulging in such an exercise, we move closer to situating our own selves within their own authentic frameworks. The people all around us either give us a boost or bring us crashing down; most often they blow up the balloon and then pop it. Here life is completely different from that of the flock of sheep. The one thing they have in common is stealing. Every day we hear that a door has had its lock broken. The hippies are not the ones responsible; it's the flock that sneaks in from the suburbs, imposing its own code of behavior on this tranquil, peaceful world. I was sure they would not be the ones to force the lock on the house I had rented; they knew that I did not own a camera or a recorder. More often than not they are aware of everything there is to know about everyone here. A young drug dealer once told me, "The people who commit these crimes don't come from Essaouira. They're all from surrounding villages. The only things the people you see around here are bothered about are hashish and women. Many people from Essaouira have met European and American women and gone away with them, never to return. That was what God wanted for them. This city has no factories, nothing. You've noticed that for yourself. Even fishing isn't all that profitable. From selling hashish, I can make double what I'd get if I went out in a fishing boat, even during a very good fishing season. Do you understand? But I'll never steal."

"I've nothing worth stealing in any case," I said.

"I'm not talking about you," he replied, "They can smell rabbits from far away, as far as their villages. They know what they're doing. But let one of them try their tricks on me. I'll rip his guts out. Neither death nor jail can stand in the face of people's honor."

With that he pulled out his knife, a real butcher's knife that gleamed in the sunlight, then put it away again. I recalled the knife in Camus's novel *The Stranger* and told myself that the French had defamed us to the world. In André Gide's *Si le grain ne meurt,* he may have said that Arabs possess something different, but Camus turned that something into a knife held in his hand. So it's all about things. Arabs have to have something to distinguish them, whatever it may be. I hope your mind can help you understand. So enough of this young man and his knife. I need to throw myself into the waves. It is ten in the morning.

The village was quiet. A woman was bending over and planting something, while another kept her face hidden from me. That's alright. Go rain somewhere else; I don't need you. What I need is sand and water.

I was strolling across the grass between the trees. A donkey raised its head and stared at me. It kept on staring;

behind it was a chicken, and beyond that a hut alongside a tree. Once I had crossed the area, I reached an open space where some twenty completely naked people were sunbathing and talking. Beyond this tree-lined space stretched the sea. It was a lovely spot. None of them paid me any attention. I followed their lead and took off my clothes. When I spotted naked female hippies playing around on the sand, I had a weird feeling. Closing my eyes, I ran toward the sea. My mouth tasted salty, and my body felt cold. After swimming for a while, I went back to my clothes pile. Stretching out on the sand, I rolled over. As I turned on to my stomach, the sand felt warm; when Eros was aroused inside me, I lay on my back with my eyes tight shut. This was something I had never actually imagined, the kind of thing you might dream about between four walls when you get back home after an exhausting day's work. You can keep on dreaming until they carry you away to your grave.

I don't mean to upset anyone. That's why I am saying that the sun was hot that morning, and so was the sand; the water was cold, my mouth tasted salty. Not only that, but we have to satisfy all her desires in order to get to the heaven from which she expelled us. She was the one who initially expelled us, and she will be the one to restore us to it if we respect her to the very end. What power! I slipped my hand into the pile of clothes and grabbed the matches. I lit her cigarette so she would admit me to heaven tomorrow on the Day of Judgment. I noticed a kind of satisfaction in her eyes, and that made me happy. At least I had guaranteed myself a place in heaven.

"Thanks," she said. "I saw you one evening at the Café Hippy. Don't you remember me?"

"No, I don't."

"I drank from your cup of tea."

"I don't remember."

"I'm sure you don't remember. You were very distracted that day. We'd all been smoking. Thanks again."

She went away and joined two other girls, along with a young man who was chatting and drawing something on the sand. I closed my eyes again. I could hear birds twittering everywhere on the trees, talk, and laughter. The hot sun was scorching my skin. Total relaxation and a craving for a long, deathlike slumber. Needless to say, I'm not sure that death really is a deep sleep, or if, once the soul departs the body, it becomes self-aware and escapes the state of unawareness that it has to endure here on earth, that thin veil that only sophists, ascetics, and prophets could tear away before their souls departed their bodies.

Resisting the urge to sleep, I jumped up from the sand and ran like a lunatic toward the sea. Once I had taken the plunge, I looked back to see whether anyone was paying any attention to me. In fact, someone was, but she was staring at me from far away and laughing. Her breasts were as white as wax. She too jumped up, ran towards me, and plunged in the water.

"Terrific!" she said. "It's so wonderful to swim with trees all around. Do you know this place? We've been coming here ever since we arrived at Essaouira."

"No, I don't know it," I replied. "I usually get to hear of places where people swim naked, but I came here just by chance."

"There's another place," she said, "but it's crowded."

"What about the gendarmes?" I asked her. "Don't they bother you?"

"I've never seen any of them here," she replied. "You should try swimming at night under the full moon. This place is Heaven itself. Why don't you come with us tonight after we've smoked some hashish at the Danish place?"

"I'll do my best."

With that I dived into the sea and watched her moving her arms through the water. She kept diving and kicking with her legs in the air. Then her head would appear again.

"Come over here," she yelled. "Every time I move forward," she added, "the weight of water on my body shifts."

I didn't listen to her. Instead I decided to surrender my body to the small waves and let them push me toward the sand; and then to do it all over again. When I didn't comply with her wishes, she came over and began doing the same thing as me. Some waves managed to make us crash into each other; at one point she managed to cling to my waist. Putting my hands on her shoulders, I pushed her down as hard as I could, but she managed to slip away with a laugh.

"Do you want to drown me?" she asked. "I don't want to die. I'm still young. There are lots of things I'd still like to see in this life."

I had no desire to kill her. Maybe she was joking, maybe not. At that particular moment at least, I could not conceive of the idea, the very notion in fact, of killing anyone, even one of my very worst enemies. I am well aware of the fact that we often feel like murdering certain people: political enemies, wives, cheating lovers, rivals, and villains. But this girl did not belong to any of those categories, so I had never thought about killing her, especially at this particular moment. I could not hurt a single soul, even though I sometimes tell myself that hurting someone is simply a reaction; and as those reactions intensify, evil consequences emerge. But this time my reaction had no evil intent; I was simply playing a joke. She laughed and plunged back into the water. I did likewise and kept my eyes open, but I could not keep it up for long. I rubbed my eyes and stood there watching as she frolicked like a seal. She kept shouting at me, but I didn't dare join her. Getting out of the water, I sat on the wet sand. The horizon was far away, and the trees extended into the distance, leaving the sun and all-pervasive quiet. When she joined me, she threw herself down by my side.

"Awesome!" she said. "The water's great. Now I'm tired."

"You swim like a shark," I told her.

"Have you ever seen one?" she asked. "They scare me."

"Only in pictures."

"Have you ever eaten shark meat?" she asked.

"I don't know. I can't remember."

She was totally naked. I tried placing my hands between my thighs to cover myself, but she did not do the same. I could feel a gentle breeze tickling the space between my thighs. I preferred to go over to where the sand was hot.

"Now I'd like a cigarette," she said. "After a swim, I really enjoy a good smoke."

"I don't have any hashish on me," I said.

"Don't worry about it," she replied, "We have a big piece. Kristin bought it yesterday."

"Have you had a good breakfast?" I asked. "You need to eat something before smoking."

"I always eat well. Don't worry about me."

She walked ahead of me. I amused myself by throwing seashells into the water, something I never used to do. For a while, I ran on the wet sand and kicked the waves with my feet. Then I decided to catch up with her. Near my clothes pile was a Moroccan girl getting undressed. I recognized her. After first she was taken aback, but after a moment's hesitation she carried on taking her clothes off. I didn't say anything to her. People said she was from Meknes, married, divorced, and now a drug dealer. Her looks kept pushing me away—another reaction—but I did not do the same. Her body looked bronzed and desirable. I told myself I could not do it with her even if they killed me. I had never seen her smile at a Moroccan. Only her husband might know why she never smiled at Moroccans. I lay down on the hot sand next to them, but said nothing. I kept peeping at the Moroccan woman's body. Her pubic hair was like a coal-black bush. A sumptuous body, not moving in the sunshine, frozen in place like a statue discarded on the beach.

"Do you smoke?" I heard a voice ask from behind me.

I grabbed the cigarette, took two quick puffs, then gave it back to the person that handed it to me without even looking behind me. I was looking straight ahead at the statue spread-eagled on the sand, totally unable to guess what she might be thinking about. I tried but failed. I could still remember the disgust she had shown at the Café Hippy whenever any Moroccan tried to approach her. The way she used to flirt with the secret police was weird; every time they wanted her, they took her away to the police station. They all desired her body, so much so that for them she became common property. She would certainly behave the same way if we were waylaid by the gendarmes between the trees. Just then she stood up and strutted proudly toward the sea.

"Do you like her?" I heard a voice behind me. "She has a beautiful body."

"No," I replied, "She's not my type."

"Even so, she's beautiful."

"If only she wanted to be one of my girlfriends!" the young man said.

"Why don't you catch up with her?" I said. "Maybe she won't say no."

As I said that, I looked at his buttocks drooping on the hot sand. As she played in the water, he kept tracking her with his eyes. As far as I could tell, not a single vein in his body was pulsing; he had been castrated long ago, and all he could do was talk—without any genuine desire. "I'm just kidding," he said. "I don't like sex without love."

"Have you ever been in love?"

"Yes, I have," he replied. "In fact, I still love one woman. I'll never love anyone else."

"You're a romantic," I replied.

"Could be," he said. "We should give our lives a different impulse. We don't have to do whatever other people do."

"That's his viewpoint," I told myself. "He may well be right."

I cannot be sure how other people used to live in the past. Books and love poems might all be that sincere. But even if they do manage to convey a picture of a specific mind-set that was current at one particular time, they cannot possibly provide any information about dead people's hidden intentions, whether they happened to be pompous, dreamers, tyrants, oppressed folk, misers, or generous patrons. Ah, me! They are all dead. It never occurred to them that they would die . . . what an awful feeling, have such thoughts about death while life is embodied right here, among trees, close to the sea, in an empty spot. Now I will go back to that bronzed body. "Here it is," I will say, "strutting before my very eyes. She walks with both poise and confidence, just like the wives of government officials in a public market. The only things she's missing are clothes and servants."

"She's the most beautiful woman I've seen here," the young man said again.

"You're right," the two girls responded in unison.

"Poor woman," I commented. "The police keep on needing her."

"Does she like that?"

"I don't know."

"If she's forced to do that, then it's dreadful, inhuman. They've no right to behave like that."

"They're the same everywhere," the young man replied. "You've no idea. Once a policeman was charged with raping a thirteen-year-old girl in Nice."

"How dreadful!" she said. "That's barbaric!"

The Moroccan woman lay down on the sand and placed her shirt over her pubic hair, leaving her breasts exposed. She did not talk to anyone, frozen once again like a statue. She might have fallen asleep. When I rested my head and closed my eyes, rainbow colors danced in front of them.

Close by someone turned on a transistor radio, and I heard soft rock music.

"Hey, look over there," one of the girls said. "Are those men shepherds? They've been staring at us for some time from behind those bushes."

I raised my head. About five bedouin were laughing behind the bushes, but the hippies were ignoring them. They just continued sunbathing, swimming, and smoking. The bedouin were not laughing out loud, but their expressions showed how shocked and upset they felt. Their eyes were gleaming brightly and seemed to be rolling in their very sockets.

"That long-haired, skinny beanpole is a Muslim like us," I heard one of them say.

Since there was no other Moroccan at this particular spot, I gathered that they were talking about me.

"Why is he naked like them?" I heard another one ask. "Maybe he's not a real man."

"I don't think it's that," another man suggested. "He's probably behaving like that so he can get one of those girls for himself. If he did that, he'd be a real Muslim. As you know, we Muslims are as virile as bulls."

I wondered what might happen. Previous experiences of mine might come into play, let alone other factors with which I was very familiar, things that these creatures spread-eagled on the sand would know nothing about.

"They're laughing at us like imbeciles," one of the girls said. "Have they never seen a naked body before? Have they never been to the hammam? Have they never slept with naked women?"

"I've no idea," I replied, "They're simple countryfolk. For them everything they see is strange."

"Why don't they behave the way we do?"

"Their traditions make that impossible. But it does not stop them doing things that are really nasty."

"Poor people!"

As soon as she said that, the men turned into demons. I watched as they vaulted their way into the area. Each one of them attacked a naked body. The whole place became a blur of sand and punches, with all the males fighting each other. I decided to beat a quick retreat. As I picked up my clothes so I could put them on in the tall grass, I did my best to cover up my private parts and protect my buttocks. Muslims like these men would be capable of doing anything, even having sex with a donkey or fish. I have even heard that in the south they do it with porcupines, then eat them later. Ugh! I saw one of the bedouin fall to the ground motionless; one of the hippies had knocked him out. The girls kept screaming beneath the men's flailing bodies. Some of them managed to get partially dressed. Two of the bedouin ran away and hid themselves somewhere, while another tried his best to fend off the kicks to his face, but without success. A group of hippies was piled up top of another of the bedouin men. I felt very anxious as I watched the whole thing, although it was exactly what I had expected to happen. The group of defeated bedouin scattered all over the area, clearly stunned by what had just happened. The last of them managed to escape toward the sea, bleeding from his neck and dragging his leg like a wounded wolf caught in a trap. I saw her there, naked and frail in the scorching sunlight. In her right hand she was holding a knife dripping with blood. As I hid in the bushes, I suddenly felt really scared.

I told myself that she could slay me like the other man. She was looking distracted. Once I could tell for certain that the knife she was holding did not belong to the "stranger" but was European, I started running crazily across the grass and through the trees till I got back to the town . . .

6

THE MESSIAH SAID, John 10:27, "My sheep listen to my voice. I know them, and they follow me." Well, I told myself, my sheep listen to my voice. I know them, but they don't follow me. Instead they sometimes turn into ravenous wolves. That is why Christ must be killed within me and turned into a sheep, wolf, or fox. I have done that many times, both night and day. Now it is daytime, and for sure it will not be like all other days. No moment bears any resemblance to any others, so how can it be with days? People who imagine that all their moments are the same are deluding themselves. From the outside, moments may look the same, but inside the human soul everything is different from one second to the next or even much less time than that.

I was sitting on a rock in front of the only store in the small town. Some of the customers were hippies who regularly used the store to buy the things they needed. They would greet people in their own languages or with gestures—a sort of familiarity. Perhaps they got into the habit of doing that in Amsterdam, Katmandu, or some London neighborhoods. I finished my sandwich—tuna fish from Safi on half bread. I also drank a Coke. I was still holding a chunk of bread, so I wrapped it up in a piece of newspaper and put it down on the wall I was leaning against. Immediately a bunch of ants started making their way, almost instinctively, toward it. After I had finished eating, I had the feeling that I needed something else and tried in vain to work out what it might be. In front of my eyes I could see a film playing: a woman, a glass of wine, a fight, a pipe, a cigarette, a joint. Eventually I lit a cigarette and took some deep puffs. I looked up. "Hello!" I said to a dirty little girl, but she ran away. She was walking barefoot on the hot sand and carrying a bottle of Oulmes water. Over the sea, the sky looked a clear blue. There were also a few white clouds, looking, as the text of the Qur'an has it, "like fluffed wool" (and God Almighty has spoken the truth, Qur'an 101:5).

Brahim was at the head of a group of hippies. When he saw me, he came over. He was chewing something that turned out to be a piece of gum.

"Teacher, what are you doing here?" he asked me. "Why haven't you gone to the beach?"

"I've just eaten," I replied. "I was very hungry."

"Good for you! When you feel hungry, you need to eat so you won't be so skinny."

The hippies behind him were stared at me silently. One of them put his arm on the shoulders of a blonde girl. She snuggled into his arms, and he kissed her forehead without saying a word. They kept looking at me.

"Have they just arrived today?" I asked Brahim.

"No," he replied, "they've come from Marrakesh. They spent last night somewhere, and since early morning I've been looking for a place for them. Can you take some of them with you? You live alone, don't you? They can pay the rent. You're just a poor teacher and you don't deal in drugs. Your paltry salary will never be enough. Beyond that, getting to know people is a treasure. Who can say, you may benefit from them. I know someone who met a hippy girl. She took him to Los Angeles, and now he's teaching Moroccan Arabic there. Imagine that. Praise God, you're educated and smart. If I had your cultural knowledge, I wouldn't have stayed here in Morocco. You can get beaten up by young men here; some of their mothers are pimps and others' sisters are whores . . ."

"That's something else, Brahim," I replied, "I'm trying to save this country."

"Who do you think you are, Teacher?" he asked. "Save yourself first. They're all building villas and apartment buildings, but all you have is squat."

"Build and build high," I retorted, "then leave it behind . . ."

"That's your business."

He turned to the group and spoke to them in French. I stood up, walked over, and stood in the middle of a group of seven, four men and three girls.

"It's hard to find a place here," one of them said.

"It depends," I replied. "People don't stay here long; just three or four days, then they leave and go somewhere else in the wide world."

"We're going to Fez too in a few days. Will you come with us?"

"No. I prefer this place. I'll stay here for a bit longer, then go back to Casablanca."

"Casablanca's huge and nasty, like any European city."

"Exactly."

We reached the house. One of them spoke French with a clear accent. I learned later that he was a German, beardless and skinny, but nice. The one who was not saying anything kept staring suspiciously at me and not smiling. He was from Belgium and looked gay; you can't miss such types. Maybe he went out to the woods later to look for a shepherd. God forbid! When we went inside, everyone put down his things as agreed. One of the girls took out a drum and started tapping on it.

"Have you ever smoked hashish in the bong?" the German asked me.

I lied. "Yes," I said.

I knew that the bong had sent a lot of people to the Barchid hospital. The young man delved into his bag and brought out a bunch of dry leaves.

"We want to try it," he said, "but we don't know how."

"It's easy. I'll show you."

"Will you smoke with us?"

"Of course," I replied.

They kept staring at the pale leaves in amazement. One of them adjusted his spectacles and started gazing at them with palpable excitement, almost like a child looking at a new toy he is discovering for the first time.

"Do you have a gas stove and teapot?" I asked the German.

"Susie," I heard another young man say, "go to the car. There's a stove there and everything else we need."

The girl disappeared. One of the young men took a look at the mud-brick walls and cast an eye around the bare room. "This is a big room," he said. "Is the rent reasonable?"

"Yes," I replied.

"We've been trying to find a place here, but with no luck. It's cheap. We've heard a lot, I mean Helen and I, about the town of Dyabat. We met the others on the road, the world road, I mean, that long road where you get to meet all kinds of people and then leave them forever. How beautiful this life is, isn't it, and yet so trivial?"

"Here's another crazy one," I told myself. "Let's test him."

"What you say makes sense. Death comes in the end, but people don't realize it. We keep each other company on a dark road in order to achieve a goal. Once we get there, we make allowances, then go our own way, and each one meets his own destiny."

"But why isn't the road bright?"

"If it were," I replied, "we wouldn't need company."

He fell silent and took a sideways glance at the girl tapping on the drum. She was not paying any attention or even aware of his glances; the others were not paying attention either. They may have been talking, either inside, about, or to their own things.

Susie came back with the gas stove and a blue teapot with a black bottom. She also brought a plastic water bottle and sugar cubes. She was wearing a red scarf, one edge of which hung between her breasts while the other was draped over her shoulder. The other girl was still drumming with the tips of her fingers, while the rest were in their own private worlds. The young German was certainly not in their world.

"Can you prepare the bong for us?" he asked, looking at me excitedly.

I pulled the gas stove close to me, then filled the teapot with water and let it boil. Actually, this was the first time I had prepared a bong. I had heard about the way to prepare things, but I was not sure about any of it.

"Try doing it the same way they used with the Hiroshima bomb," the fox suggested, "the way the first bomb was tested, the way every evil human intention has been tested throughout history."

"I'll do it," I told the fox calmly. When I noticed steam rising from the teapot, I added a handful of dry leaves. This time the group did not remain imprisoned in their own private worlds; instead they were all eagerly awaiting the result.

"Shall we have it in cups," Susie asked, "or straight from the teapot? Should we sniff it or drink it?"

"No," I told her, "we should drink it in cups, just like tea or coffee. I forgot to mention that."

"I'll go and get some plastic cups from the car," she said.

I took the lid off the teapot; the leaves were changing color and bubbling slowly. Once the color had completely changed, the fox spoke to me.

"Since you're not sure of what you're doing, that's enough. Be careful. With every first experience you need to be careful. You need to bear in mind that the shepherd always stands behind the lamb or ewe."

I turned off the gas and waited for Susie to bring the cups. She did not take long. The fox instructed me to take the lead, so I complied. I poured a few drops into my own cup, then into the others'. They were all waiting for someone to start. I realized that no one was willing to risk his or her life. With a feigned self-confidence, I pretended that there was nothing unusual about what we were doing; it was all completely normal. We were simply drinking a plant with no particular effect; it might well make them feel happy and bring them close to that absolute joy they so desired. I had no idea whether such absolute happiness actually existed. They all looked hesitant; some of them kept sniffing the cups like animals that smell their food before devouring it. I did not sniff my own cup but brought it to my lips and took a small, noisy sip, albeit cautiously and with a certain anxiety. I noticed that some of them were still holding the cups close to their noses and lips without daring to take sip. I took a second loud sip, laughing and faking utter delight as I did so. Finally, one of them took a sip form his cup. When they asked him how it tasted, he told them it was terrific, very nice indeed. He took another sip. I made a point of taking very noisy sips, and eventually everyone else all did the same. It all proceeded naturally.

"This beats coffee or tea," one of them said.

"Certainly," one the girls agreed, "it tastes nice. Unfortunately, I've never heard of this kind of bong."

"I will be watching you, you monkey!" I said without thinking.

"What did you say?" she asked.

"What are you saying?" the fox asked me. "Are you crazy? Talk to her in her own language."

"The bong's great," I told her. "In a while, you're going to feel really happy. We'll all be hovering over an amazing imaginary world."

"Is that true?" another of them asked.

"You'll see."

One of them lay down on the mat, unable to say another word; he was staring at nothing in particular, looking around aimlessly. Not long afterwards, the others were doing the same. One after another, they fell asleep. I too began to feel sleep coming on. My eyelids felt heavy. After taking a few more noisy sips, I put the cup down in front of me. I could feel something crawling over my body and head and taking control.

"So this is the kind of effect the bong has on you," I told myself. "It's a strong sleeping pill. If I'd drunk my whole cup, I'd be asleep by now just like them."

I did not fall asleep but had a strange sensation unlike the one I feel when I drink wine, or smoke hashish or kif. I was left on my own in the room-hut. All around me and in front of me the "people of the cave" were sleeping. I felt scared. I listened as one of them snored like a pig. Another one was lying on his stomach and mumbling nonsense. I leapt to my feet as though I had been stung. As I charged out of the room, I knocked my cup with my foot and spilled everything. I wanted to ask the fox for help, but it had disappeared. I was surprised that it could let me down in a situation like this. I ran and ran; houses, trees, dirt, silence, voices, vacuum, wilderness, trees, sand, sea, sun. Amid the waves, I felt as though I were dragging a heavy bag. My soaking wet clothes felt heavy on me. I stumbled into the water, but in vain, trying desperately to recover my normal state so I could be rid of this crawling sensation and languor. Leaving the water, I felt utterly exhausted and threw myself down on the sand under the scorching hot sun. I had no sense of the people around me; instead I fell asleep and only woke up around dusk. There were a few human ghosts to be seen, moving far away along the beach. I looked all around me and began to muster a few of the pictures and images I had seen during my sleep; there were so many of them and they were so weird that I did not succeed. I could feel that my clothes were still wet. Shaking off the sand, I still did not feel cold. I walked to the village and found it almost deserted. I felt hungry and went to the store where the owner spotted me.

"Were you at today's farce?" he asked.

"I'm starving." I told him, "I need a *casse-croûte* or anything. I need food."

"You must have smoked a lot of hashish. Thank God you're not one of those crazies. They wrecked the town."

"Who?"

"Those hippies who arrived today. They must have used a bong. Everyone said that only the bong could make them do that."

"If that's what they took," I asked, "surely people knew how to bring them back to their senses, didn't they?"

The hippies had tried to set fire to some houses. One of them had jumped on an old woman, grabbed the knife she was using to clean a goat's skin to make a canteen, and used it to rip the skin in pieces. He almost killed her, so she ran off and asked her son-in-law for help. Then the villagers came out and attacked the hippies with sticks. The hippies made for the woods like so many wolves. As I listened to this tale of the bong, I kept swallowing without chewing. If I had drunk all of my cup, I would have ended up like them.

"Bravo!" I told the fox. "That's great work you've done! That's how I always want you to behave."

"Go check your things," the fox instructed me, "and hitch a ride on the first kind of transport that arrives. Leave the village and head for Essaouira. Have a bottle of wine when you get there, but don't smoke any hashish tonight. Things may end up badly. Make sure your lambs can hear your voice."

"A great idea," I replied.

I paid the store owner and left.

7

WAS IT FATIMA who had disappeared or had I? In a small store with a very old mat on the floor, there she was, sitting in the corner. There were a few other people sitting on the mat, eating and smoking hashish or kif. When she spotted me, she jumped up.

"Ali!" she said. "I've missed you, handsome! Where have you been all this time? I left Essaouira for a few days and came back. I like this weather. It seems I can't live anywhere else in the world. Come over and sit with us."

She pointed toward a young man who looked as though he came from a wealthy family. He was staring at me silently. His clothes were not dirty yet; no doubt, he was new to this lifestyle. We stepped over some feet and heads and sat down on the mat facing the young man.

"This is Ali," Fatima told him. "He's a teacher in Casablanca."

The young man nodded his head without uttering a word. His red eyes kept staring the door of the store. He had obviously smoked a lot of hashish or maybe something even stronger. Maybe I was wrong; perhaps he was not a drug addict or from a wealthy family.

"I haven't seen you in a while," Fatima said.

"I'm always in either Essaouira or Dyabat. Sometimes it's better to disappear for a while so you can discover other worlds or your own self."

"That's true," she replied. "You're always talking about complex issues, to the extent that humans can think logically about such things. I always remember the things you say. But don't you actually think I'm stupid and don't understand anything?"

"I've never said that."

She turned to the young man who was still staring at the store door and the paint on the wall opposite.

"Azeddine," she asked him, "do you still have a joint?"

The young man remained silent and frozen in place. Putting his hand in his jacket pocket, he calmly took out a pack of American cigarettes and something else and handed them to Fatima. At this point, the proverbial Hind fulfilled her promise even though she had never promised us anything, nor had we ever asked her for anything.

"I don't live in hotels anymore," she told us. "I live in a house owned by Azeddine in the old Mellah. We have an enjoyable time there with some of his friends and a few other male and female drop-ins."

As usual, Azeddine stared silently at her. His hair hung down to his shoulders, black and clean. I remembered that I had not washed in a while; that is why I had not slept well and kept tossing and turning in bed—especially in the morning when the effects of alcohol and hashish wore off. I started scratching and felt extremely hot at specific spots on my body. I could also smell the sea blended with whatever my pores were discharging. Apparently Azeddine had a bathhouse inside the place that Fatima was talking about. He kept smoking heavily in front of me. The smoke inside the store had a hard time making it outside; it lingered, twisting and twirling in the darkened space.

"Yesterday night was great," Fatima continued, "wasn't it, Azeddine?"

Looking up, the young man finally said something.

"Yes, it was," he replied, "apart from that stupid Dutch girl who was trying to kill herself when she started banging her head against the wall. But we're used to such things here."

"Are you from Essaouira?" I asked him.

"Yes," he replied deliberately, "I'm from Essaouira, and the house where I live belongs to my grandfather. We live in Casablanca."

"You must be a student."

"Yes, I am. In French literature, but I don't like it. There aren't any decent teachers. If it weren't for my handicapped mother, I'd have gone to France, Switzerland, or Belgium to study. But the poor woman keeps clinging to me because I'm the only boy in the family. All my four sisters are married. I only tolerate studying in Rabat for her sake. I don't go to all the lectures. I prefer reading at home."

"That's fine. Many geniuses were autodidacts. Departments of humanities don't produce *littérateurs*."

"I'm well aware of that. When the break's over, we'll see. By then my mother may have died, and then I'll go away to write a PhD on Jacques Audiberti's drama."

Fatima stood up, and I watched her as she started yelling something by the door. The light inside the store turned dark, and a group of hippies, men and women, gathered around her. A woman passed by, enveloped in a *hayik* with only her left eye visible. She was using that single eye to stare at Fatima. No doubt she was saying to herself, "God forbid, what a whore! Prostitution should have its own rules: seclusion, prestige, pride, and a sense of honor, and so on . . ."

Fatima came back inside trailed by a barefoot, dirty hippy with pants torn at the knee and his rear end on display like a white piece of fat.

"This is Gunter," she said. "He's a nice young man."

"He was with us one night," Azeddine said. "Stop bringing people like this. He's crazy. We don't want anything to do with lunatics."

"Hello!" Gunter said.

He used a rubber band to tie up his ponytail. Azeddine did not respond to his greeting and turned in my direction.

"These hippies are all we need!" he said. "If I'm going to be spending my own money, I need to know who I'm spending it on—certainly not people like this idiot. Some hippies are very smart; they can talk about everything, literature, art, and philosophy. But no one can understand what this man is talking about; it's just that he can eat like a ravenous ghoul. Just imagine, that night he managed to eat the contents of an entire cooking pot without even washing his dirty nails."

"You're right. I don't like these hollow types either."

"But the poor guy's kind and nice," Fatima said.

"Because he's as ignorant as you are," was Azeddine's reply.

I was surprised to hear him say that. I could see Fatima burning the store down on the spot and destroying everything. But the words were stuck in her throat. She simply sucked it all up and said nothing.

"Aha!" I thought, "so here's an example of human ambiguity: lion and ostrich, good and evil, courage and cowardice."

I remembered when she had told me that she was a Zemouri girl, and that I should never forget it. But with human nature the way it is now, there's no more Zemouri, Doukkali, or Fassi. Human beings have just as much in common as they are different. Fatima had turned into a weak ewe in its postpartum period; she had surrendered to the shepherd. But I knew full well that she was hiding the viper inside her just as I was hiding my own fox, surveying everything going on with a quiet prudence. That trait is also to be found with foxes: a coward at times, withdrawing when it senses danger, but at others a ferocious assailant.

"It's okay," I told Azeddine. "Let him stay with us until he makes up his own mind to leave. At any rate, he looks high enough!"

"High or not," Azeddine replied, "he's not going to sniff any of my hashish. I'm prepared to spend all the capital from my father's factory on smart people, but people like him make me uncomfortable. They're simply a burden."

"Don't tell me we're going to take him home with us again." Azeddine told Fatima.

"I didn't say that," Fatima replied. "In any case, it's not my house."

As the ewe made that statement, her masculine side disappeared. I now saw her as a real female. The image of her I had in my mind, the one from our first encounter, changed. Meanwhile Gunter was not paying any attention to what was going on between us. He kept looking around at the hippies inside the place who were either eating or smoking hashish. He waved at a girl in the distance, and she smiled back at him. He moved a little forward on the mat, and Azeddine moved back in disgust, looking at me in the hope that I shared his feelings.

"What do you do?" I asked Gunter.

"I'm touring the world," he replied.

"Did you quit school for that reason?"

"I've been a student in a youth detention center," he replied in broken French. "My last school was two years in an Iranian jail. I like the Iranian shah; he's a great man. But jail there is brutal."

"Do you hear what this pig is saying?" Azeddine asked. "How can you learn anything from him?"

"That's okay." I told Azeddine, "We should learn how to listen to everyone. From their mistakes, we can learn how to deal with our own."

"The very existence of such people on this planet of ours is a grave mistake."

"How do you know?" I asked him. "Maybe it's our existence that's the mistake, by which I mean the minority."

He let his thoughts wander through the smoke in the place. Without any further comment, he told Fatima to roll him another joint.

"Oh! You've some hashish," Gunter said with delight. "Great, fantastic!"

"I swear to God," Azeddine said in Arabic, "your lips are never going to touch this cigarette."

"Don't worry," said Fatima, "I'll get rid of him politely."

"That's your business."

But the way she sent him away was not very polite. "Gunter," she told him, "I'll see you later. We need to discuss some personal things now."

"Okay, okay," he replied quite spontaneously. "I'll see you at the Café Hippy."

"Sure."

"Good-bye," he said.

Stepping over some heads and feet, he left the store. I heard Azeddine heave a sigh of relief.

"Don't do that again," he told Fatima.

"I didn't realize you hated him." she replied. "I won't do it again."

"You know I like to choose my own friends."

"My apologies," he said turning in my direction. "I don't mean you. I'm talking that way about those hippies because I know them so well. You're welcome to stay in my house. You shouldn't worry. Food, booze, hashish, and girls are on me from now on. People like us are rare around here."

"Thanks," I replied, "but I'm living in Dyabat now."

"Leave your hut there and come stay with us. But you seem to prefer isolation."

"It's a strange world there; that's why I've preferred to explore it. Maybe I can store something in my memory, so at some point in the future I can write a novel or something about that world."

"Great! Do you write?"

"A few short stories," I replied.

"I'm a writer too. I write poetry, but I don't publish it. I'll read to you later. This girl doesn't understand such things, but she's a great cook even though she cheats."

The music blared all of a sudden, Jimi Hendrix's voice. I recognized it at once, unmistakable. Azeddine's body shuddered; he was no longer as rigid as he had been. His expression changed suddenly, and he looked much more cheerful. I never realized music could have that effect on a human being. Azeddine now turned into someone else: strong, engaging, and daring. Fatima rolled the joint gently between her hands, then lit it and handed it to him. He inhaled, then handed it to me. Guitar sound was filling the whole place, insinuating its way amid the kif smoke in the air and maybe extending to the outside space as well.

"Hendrix is a creative genius," Azeddine said. "He's a writer, and he writes with the guitar. He paints extraordinary paintings and hovers in dream space, especially when you're high listening to him."

Nodding in agreement, I passed the cigarette to Fatima. Closing my lips, I gave the smoke that I had breathed in a chance to circulate deep inside this body that belonged neither to the fox nor to me.

I used to get this feeling a lot, imagining the body as a mere cart for carrying something that might be the soul. But the soul is part of God's purview, and so it might be something else. By now the smoke was permeating the cart's turning wheels in order to squeeze whatever that particular thing might be. I told myself that the body was simply a tool for defending that thing, the one that exists in everything, even in the sound of the guitar. The body is a shield, whether it's this body of mine or any other bodies of living creatures. That other thing, the one that might be called the soul—by which I mean the human soul, animal soul, the soul of scent, of sound, of sunshine, of the entire universe, which can only be God—that other thing is very strange indeed. If we proceed through the eternal labyrinth, it can only lead to one of two things: denial or proof, doubt or certainty.

"What are you thinking about?" Azeddine asked. "I feel I'm in a special state. Do you?"

"Me too." I replied. "Sometimes I feel bewildered, and it makes me nervous. I withdrew from the rest of the flock."

"Do you call people a flock?" Azeddine asked. "Bravo! They really are a flock."

"Every time I smoke hashish or kif, my throat feels dry and I get hungry."

"Ask for some lemonade," Azeddine suggested. "Anything you want. I told you not to worry about anything. I realize you're a poor teacher. I'm sure you also have a family to take care of. Don't think I'm stupid and don't understand such things."

"I've some money. I'll go and get a beer."

"Good idea," he said. "Why don't you ask us to drink with you? Do you think I'm a bigot in a lion's skin?"

With that, Azeddine stood up and paid the store-owner. We went to a small bar that he knew well. Fatima was drinking in silence. She had completely changed; the quick temper that I knew her for had totally vanished. Azeddine was not the kind of man to play the lapdog in front of women. He was tough and nice at the same time. In the short time I'd known him, I'd noticed that he had a lot of self-confidence, the very thing that the flock lacked. The image I'd created of him at first—a spoiled, stupid, rich boy with no confidence in either himself or other people—had completely disappeared. It was only now that I realized why he was so taciturn and shy. The silence was simply a process of observation, a preliminary assessment before making a move or saying a word. Even so, I felt he was at ease with me. At the very least he had found someone to whom he could talk about his project—Jacques Audiberti as a playwright. Any discussion of such things with other people would be a kind of insanity. In this frigid land of Morocco, people usually only talk about their vaginas and the houses or farms they will own. In such cases, people like Azeddine have no choice but to remain silent, to listen and contemplate their own internal pains, and all because the flock is becoming more and more stupid and degenerate, desiring to forcibly impose such values on the minority that has its own sufferings to bear in addition to those of the flock.

"The same again. Very cold."

"Coming up!" the waiter replied.

"Could you get us some sardines, please?" Azeddine asked.

He looked at me. "You were going to celebrate by yourself," he said, "but why don't we have a drink together?"

"I didn't think you . . ." I replied, and then paused. "Sometimes I have reservations about humanity; in fact, not sometimes, but always . . ."

"That's the way I am as well," Azeddine said. "She was the one who introduced us to each other. I don't know a thing about this female."

"I didn't realize," Fatima said.

"And when in your life have you ever known anything?" Azeddine asked her.

No room for surprise. I watched as she gazed at the bar and then stretched out her hand out to bring the beer glass to her mouth. The waiter brought us three cold beers. In the various corners of the bar, fishermen were drinking wine and talking quietly; they are undoubtedly kept on a tight rein by the local authorities. By contrast in Casablanca, even shoeshiners can drink; when they have drunk half a bottle of wine, they can behave like caids, mayors, or ministers. It is only when they wake up in a police station cell or else with their heads in bandages after a fight involving a knife, bottle, or cup, that they assume their true personalities . . .

After the second beer, I started to feel good. Azeddine seemed happy as well. He told Fatima to roll another joint.

"Before the evening's over," I told him, "we're going to be out of it."

"Genuine consciousness can only be lost via wine or hashish," he told me, "whereas fake consciousness is still fake without any need to get drunk. But that only becomes clear when someone has something to drink or gets stoned. What I mean is that we're going to feel really tired this evening. Even so, I adore the night world; through it, I can enter the absolute. If we carry on like this, the night may well slip through my fingers."

"Don't worry," he said. "As long as you're with me, you won't miss anything. I know the town and everything that happens here. Don't worry. If you get tired, you can go to sleep. I told you that my house is yours. And don't tell me you're planning to go back to Dyabat tonight."

The waiter brought three more cold beers without being asked and opened them with a professional waiter's normal dexterity.

"Why did you do that?" Azeddine asked the waiter. "Why put yourself to so much trouble?"

"When your father owned this bar, sir," he replied, "days were good. I owe you for that."

"I've got money," Azeddine said. "Don't trouble yourself."

"May God give you more. It's no bother. I owe you. . . ."

"Your father owned this bar?" I asked Azeddine.

He nodded, then turned toward Fatima who was staring in amazement at some pictures on the wall to the left of the bar.

"Drink your beer," he told her. "We'll go home. It's 5 p.m. You can cook us a tasty tagine in the teacher's honor. The best thing you've done in your life is to introduce me to a friend whose friendship may well last for a lifetime."

"Not at all!" I replied. "I hope that's what happens. We may actually have the same temperament. In any case, it's a distinct advantage for us to share the same degree of suffering in this flock-based society."

"Once again, I assure you they really are a flock. Only a fox can live among them."

I shifted my backside on the stool; my bushy tail was about to rip my pants. Touching my nose and mouth, I sneezed. Everything stayed the same; no snout or tail appeared. Thank God for that at least; it would have given the game away, and right in front of a young man who respects me. I realized that the fox had selected a particular place and hidden itself there.

"It's better for you this way," I told myself. "You're the example. Come out and hide, both at the appropriate moment. Please don't give me away."

I watched the fox in its chosen spot as it opened its eyes in a clearly languid fashion, then closed them again.

"Tonight," I heard the ewe telling me, "I'm going to prepare the best tagine you've ever tasted."

"I didn't know you were such a good cook!"

"How long were we together," she asked, "so you could have known that much about me?"

"It's better for you not to know her," Azeddine said. "She's a cheat and thinks she's smarter than everyone else."

Azeddine's words made her laugh; she was apparently not offended. I watched as he drank his beer in one swallow, then got up calmly.

"Let's go" he said. "We need to have everything ready before dark."

I did as he said, but Fatima needed help. We left the bar and walked along narrow alleys, some empty, others crowded with people. We reached an old-fashioned door with a bronze door knocker. Rather than knock on the door, Azeddine chose to give it a kick. We climbed a stone staircase and found ourselves in a wide living room with a colorful Moroccan carpet on the floor.

"Feel free," Azeddine told me. "Your room is over there. Do you want to look at it now?"

"Later," I said. "Thanks."

"The girl sleeps with me in my room," he went on. "We usually sleep in the living room. As you already know, when you stay up late, you never know how or where you slept."

"That's happened to me many times," I told him.

"I slept in a dumpster once," Azeddine said, "after I'd been bothered by some idiots."

"Me too. It's weird how similar our lives have been!"

Just then the fox spoke to me. "Don't exaggerate just to please him."

"Okay," I replied.

"What's that you're saying?" Azeddine asked.

"I said I'd had the same experience," I told him, "and that it was weird."

"Please take a seat," said Azeddine. "That box over there is full of wine bottles. If you want to smoke or listen to some music, feel free. I'll be out for a minute."

Fatima was sitting in front of me, leafing through some magazines that were scattered all over the carpet. Actually, she was not sitting, but rather lying on her stomach.

"Take good care of the teacher," Azeddine told Fatima while he was still standing there. "If he wants to eat, you're familiar enough with the kitchen. If anyone I respect comes, let him in. But I don't want any crazy or stupid people inside this house."

With that, Azeddine left. Fatima stood up and turned on the stereo cassette player—Nina Simone's soft voice. I had no objections, and lay down on my back. As I smoked, I stared at the ceiling. Soon afterwards I fell asleep and only woke up when I heard Azeddine's voice.

"Let the teacher rest," he was saying. "Don't wake him up."

There were other voices too, along with music and the smell of kif and hashish.

When I opened my eyes, I found the living room crowded with male and female hippies. No one looked at me or paid me any attention. I liked that; it was very unusual. When I spotted a hippy stretched out on the floor, either sound asleep or high on hashish, I felt even more relaxed. No one was paying any attention to anyone else. Opening my eyes wide, I continued checking on the situation I was in. Azeddine was sitting next to my head, without observing or paying attention to anyone. He seemed to be chatting to someone on his right.

"Have you had enough rest?" he asked me.

"Yes, thanks, quite enough," I replied. "I've no idea how I came to fall asleep."

"You were probably exhausted from the night before last night."

"I really don't know."

"Do you want a drink or smoke?"

"I need to go to the bathroom first. I'm still in a different world."

"Which one?" Azeddine asked. "You're still in our world. As for that other world, I don't know how it will deal with this entire flock, the one that's faded away and died, and the one that's still alive."

"When I've washed my face, I'll try to blend in. You've certainly tried it yourself."

In the bathroom, Fatima kept grabbing me by the hair.

"Sleepyhead! Wake up! You won't be able to get to sleep tonight. I tried to wake you up, but Azeddine kept stopping me. I was telling him that you won't be able to get to sleep tonight."

"It doesn't matter. I'm used to that. I love watching the dawn light at the beach."

She left me alone. I put my head under the tap; drops of water ran down my back, and I felt refreshed. I had had enough of pouring water over my head, so I dried my hair with a clean towel that was hanging on the door.

"Now you're a different human being," the fox told me. "I must let you behave the way you want."

I asked myself how I can want anything; for that matter, how can anyone on earth want anything? I worked out that the flock is what decides for us what we want. Oh, how I wish that just a small percentage of what the flock wants could be realized during the course of this life! It never stops wanting and stays that way until it has to depart for the great divide without ever achieving all the things it wants. Genuine will involves what is good. Evil will is whatever the flock can manage to achieve; it exerts every possible effort to bring it about. Forgive me if I'm mixing apples and oranges here; words inevitably invoke other words. Let me go back to the bathroom, blow my nose, run the tap again, wash my face, and get back to telling the story of what happened.

Fatima came back to the bathroom and pushed the door open.

"Are you sleeping in there?" she asked. "You're taking a while."

"I was blowing my nose," I replied.

"When we were kids, we used to eat our snot," she said. "It was salty and tasted good. Whenever I did it, my mother used to hit me."

"How disgusting!" I said, "A girl shouldn't talk like that."

"What's wrong with it?" she asked. "I'm not showing off. All Moroccan girls have eaten their snot when they were younger, but now they're not proud of it. They have eaten worse things than that. I knew some of my friends who've done that before, but now they have jobs, they dress nicely and have learned how to speak French. I'm not like them. Why should I lie to you? Will you marry me?"

"Get out," I said. "I need to pee."

"Okay. It was Azeddine who sent me."

She disappeared. I made a few gesticulations in the air inside the bathroom, feeling as though I had been born anew—a feeling that human beings only experience on rare occasions. Such moments will sometimes pass without anyone even noticing; so instead of people taking advantage of them, they flit away amid the mechanical mayhem of life in the flock. Such moments as these are happy ones, and I'm well-aware that they never last. Some emergency will crop up and ruin everything; at least, that is what my past experiences have taught me. So let these be moments of precious clarity.

From the other side of the door, I heard Fatima's voice piercing through the loud music. "Ali! Come on! Your glass is waiting."

I went back to the living room and sat in the spot where I had stretched out before. The door leading to the stairs was ajar. In the corner of the room, I noticed Salma; I could not believe my eyes. I told Azeddine that I knew her, and he responded that she was stupid, although that did not stop her from being beautiful.

"Do you want her?" he asked. "Go over to her then."

"She knows me. She's slept with me. It looks as though she hasn't noticed me yet."

"She showed up with those three men while you were in the bathroom."

I kept looking at her while sipping from the glass that Azeddine had handed me. The wine had a particular taste to it, a bit strange. I lit a cigarette, still staring straight at Salma. Eventually she raised her head and looked over in my direction. She stared hard at me through the haze of kif and hashish smoke to make sure she was not mistaken. Then she actually stood up, walked over, and threw herself on me without anyone noticing. Azeddine was the only one who looked at her, but he soon went back to the world of the living room.

"Ali! Where did you disappear?" she asked me. "I've been searching for you."

"Have you come from the town?" I asked.

"Yes, with some friends. I left a party there."

"It's better for people to change location from time to time."

"You're right," she replied. "And people as well. That's what I've always tried to do."

"Me too. But I rarely change women until they decide to drop me."

"As far as I'm concerned, when it comes to places and men, it's all easy and feasible."

I asked Azeddine to pour her a glass of wine. He told me that she did not drink but occasionally smoked hashish. I asked him to double-check that she was not lying. When he handed her the glass of wine, she refused and said she preferred to smoke. He brought her a pipe from somewhere; she seemed to have been smoking a lot of hashish earlier on. I could not possibly be wrong on that score, especially since I had only just woken up. I was wavering between a desire to join the group and a lingering wish to lag behind. But what was the point of lagging behind? It was nighttime, when only God Himself could see me. At such a time no one knows me; only God is aware that I have a fox inside me. Friends and relatives who know you (or claim to know you well) are precisely the ones to wake up the fox inside you, however hard you try to keep it hidden. At moments like this, all the fox has to do is to relax and sleep. If it needs to wake up, the task will not be as difficult as we might imagine.

Back to the start. . . . Hours passed, and I started to feel drunk. I danced by myself and with others. Everything merged, by which I mean mouths with mouths, hands with breasts, or whatever. The music kept repeating itself, and the room was filled with smoke. People arrived, and others left. Azeddine disappeared from the living room, and Salma fell asleep next to a bottle of wine, which I managed to empty even though I felt I'd already had enough.

"This is a world one should write about," I thought. "Students at school need to read about it."

I realized that I was tired of teaching poetic eulogies written for caliphs and kings, and stories about the fat cat and the skinny cat, and the affectionate mother who helps her son put his clothes on and brush his teeth with toothpaste.

"Give Mommy a kiss," she tells him.

I had noticed that the majority of students have pale faces. They have rotten teeth from smoking kif, they usually don't eat breakfast, and their mother does not help them get dressed. Oh! So why precisely should we be writing about the world of hashish? Why not instead about the genuinely miserable life they lead? For example, the mother who every single morning goes to the stand and waits for someone to hire her. The man whose bicycle has been stolen. The father with two wives and ten children. The sister who prostitutes herself to help her children and siblings. How hard it is to write about this country! I imagine that, if Hemingway had been born in Ben Mssik, he would have been a shoeshiner. If Henry Miller had been born in Hayy Muhammadi, he would have probably become a cobbler. Why am I wandering off topic like this? Let me start again from where I left off. Where is the fox, and where is its tail?

I got drunk and had no desire to stay in this environment. Whenever I drink, I sometimes have an overwhelming desire to be alone. I was not blending with that world anymore.

Azeddine returned.

"What's the matter with you?" he asked as he came over. "Are you drunk? That's what we all dream about, isn't it?"

"No," I replied, "I'm not drunk. I just want to be left alone."

"Go to the next room. Do you want to take this dead body with you?"

"No need to wake her up. She's dreaming of her parents, for sure."

"Wake her up."

With that Azeddine grabbed her by the armpits. She opened her bleary eyes.

"Go to the next room," he told her, "and sleep with the teacher."

"Okay," she said.

Leaning on each other, we both headed for the next room, but we fell down twice and had to get up again. Her body felt heavy, and my feet refused to bear my weight. We lay down on the floor. She kissed me and then closed her eyes. I lit a cigarette and lay on my back, staring up at the ceiling. My head was spinning with many ideas: images, fancies, hallucinations, and violence. I stayed on the floor for a while, but then the sound of music grew louder. The door was opened, and two other people high on hashish came into the same room where I was lying on the floor with Salma. First one collapsed on the floor, then the other. One of them pointed at Salma and began talking to me. I told myself he must have known her before and gave him a nod. I let my fingers play with her hair, and he started doing the same thing with his friend's hair. They started kissing each other.

"Maybe one of them thinks the other one is female," I told myself.

However, they ended up taking their pants off. I felt disgusted and rapidly regained consciousness; I did not feel drunk anymore. I staggered to my feet and went to look for Azeddine. He came in and saw what was going on.

"Relax," he told me. "Don't bother about it. It's normal."

"I cannot tolerate such a scene. 'God created them, both male and female.' If this kind of thing was supposed to be normal, God would have created another male from Adam's rib. That way things would be settled."

"Why such philosophy, teacher?!" Azeddine asked. "Just protect your own ass, and that's it."

"But I don't like to witness such things."

"So how can you write if you don't see everything?"

"What I've seen is more than enough. In fact, I can't even write about the things I've seen. Please let me leave and sleep in Dyabat."

"For heaven's sake!" Azeddine said. "You're planning to walk all the way to the town in the early morning when it's still dark?"

"I'll walk along the beach," I replied. "I know a road that leads to the town."

"I know that road too, but someone might mug you."

"I'll have my fox with me."

"What? Are you crazy? A fox? The booze must be getting to you. It would be better for you to get some sleep now. I'll kick everyone out."

While we were talking, the two men kept panting, and then they relaxed on the floor.

"Ugh!" I said.

"So you see?" Azeddine said. "Just a fleeting, trivial moment, and it's over. The same thing will happen to you with the person sleeping next to you."

He kicked them out of the room and left me standing there. I punched the wall with my fist and cursed something in thin air. Eventually however, I wrapped myself around Salma's body. I kept picturing what might be possible and impossible, and that way I fell asleep without even doing the thing that Azeddine had pictured me doing.

8

RAYS OF SUNSHINE poke their way through the fluffy clouds that blanket city and sea. When they disperse, others take their place, and the sun's rays take up the challenge again. This is obviously the way things have been for millions of years; clouds, sun, and sea have all remained undefeated. Humans, however, have been defeated, as has human creativity, so often lauded, especially by their ancestors. Clouds, however, may dissolve but only to reform, whereas humans leave behind them water, fire, air, dirt, and desire.

Yes, desire!

I was having breakfast at 1 p.m. in the Café de France . . . coffee with milk and a croissant. When he stood in front of me, I did not recognize him at first.

"Teacher," he said. "I'm Brahim. Are you drunk? You certainly smoke and drink a lot."

"Have a seat," I said.

"Here are your things. You left them behind when you left. Obviously you don't know Essaouira and Dyabat."

"People won't steal them," I said.

He sat down but looked awkward, neither standing nor sitting.

"I need to talk to you about something," he said. "We need to leave the café at once and go somewhere else. It concerns both you and me. Otherwise you're going to spend the rest of your life in jail."

I was utterly horrified. Even if he were joking or in a hashish trance, I was still shaking with fear. In any case, he still had my things; that much could not be a joke, even though it might perhaps be a hallucination. He shouldered his bag, and we crossed the square and walked past the bus station.

"If it's something really serious," I said, "let's go down to the rocks."

"We're not going anywhere they know."

I searched for my fox's muzzle and tail, but in vain. That's how the fox can let you down at the most awkward moment. We walked until we reached Sidi Majdoul's tomb. He led me through some trees, interspersed with a few small huts and small white houses shaped like roc's eggs. There was no sign of human beings, although I may have spotted a donkey or chicken. I really don't know. We sat down by a bunch of small trees behind which there extended a vast, infertile plain.

"Now no one can possibly find out where we are," Brahim said. "We haven't done anything, but the government is merciless."

"I'm no smuggler," I said. "And you know that selling drugs is legal; that's how you make your living."

"That's not what I mean, teacher. Now let me be frank with you. We're alone here, and no one can hear us. They've found the bodies of three female hippies in the woods."

"And what's that to do with us?" I asked. "Did we kill them?"

"You don't know a thing. Sometimes things happen, and the gendarmes in Dyabat and the police in Essaouira bring in all the hippies. You don't know that. People I know personally have been often convicted for things they didn't do. Severe sentences. I beg you, take me with you to Casablanca. Save me and yourself as well. I won't bother you; I'll stay with you for just a day or two. I have some European friends who are hashish dealers there. I'll spend a day or two looking for them, then I'll leave you alone."

"I don't understand any of this," I said. "Besides I haven't killed anyone."

"I've told you; you don't know them. They'll take you; they'll take us all and hang us. They've done it to us many times before for absolutely nothing. And what about murder? Do you think they'll have more respect for you because you're a teacher? I know a teacher who took a vacation here before you. They took him to the station, and he stayed there a week cleaning it up for them. Poor man! They shaved his head. He swore he'd never come back to this city. But they won't be shaving your head; they'll be chopping it off instead."

He ran his hand across his neck. I stared at the vast infertile plain, then at the sky. No one: no human beings, no animals, only silence, interrupted by the sound of birds chirping in the branches. It seemed to me that I had seen a donkey or a chicken a while ago; I don't remember. I lit a cigarette and handed one to Brahim. No one, I told myself, wants to have problems, even a masochist. Many people are eager to tag other people with them so they can watch the fun—the kind of thing a slave wishes for his master, the housemaid for her mistress, and the abandoned lover for the one who has left. I do not want any problems; I've only ever accepted them grudgingly even when my own will has been the culprit. I don't even clean my own room in Casablanca, so how am I supposed to clean the police station or gendarmerie?

"What are you thinking about?" Brahim asked. "I know you're very smart, but I also know things that you don't. I know those sons of bitches all too well. What's happened is a mess, a full-scale mess! It is stupid for us to stick around here when God has endowed us with a brain to think with. Let's get out of here. Arrests have already started in Dyabat, and they'll soon get to Essaouira. If we stay here, we're doomed, and I'll leave the rest to your imagination. I know them. I know them all too well."

A fig fell from the tree under which we were sitting. Brahim picked it up, cleaned it, and peeled it carefully, all the while talking about what would happen to us if we were arrested by the gendarmes or the police. We shared the fig and ate it.

"Now we've shared food," he said, smacking his lips. "I'm not lying or trying to betray you. If I do, then this fig that we've just shared will have its effect on my knees. I'll never walk from now on. On my eyes too, and I'll never see again."

"May God save and preserve you," I replied, "and keep you safe for your mother."

Since this was the situation, I decided that we should cut our hair right away and clean ourselves up a bit, then travel to Casablanca by whatever means. I shared that plan with Brahim, and he suggested that we should walk some of the way until we reached a barber near a gas station where trucks regularly stop. Once again, I always want to avoid problems for myself or other people. When other people have often been hurt, it has been because of circumstances beyond my control. I am neither god nor angel.

We made our way across a small valley so we could start walking along the main road. There were no trees apart from some greenery visible in the distance. In the middle of the greenery were some whitish spots; parallel to the road was a ditch. I told myself that, if we spotted anything that looked like a gendarmes' jeep, we would throw ourselves into the ditch and hide. When I told Brahim, he said that, as long as we were far away from the town, it did not really matter anymore. All I had to do was to follow his lead, "hearing and obeying"; my only task was to take him with me to Casablanca. I told myself that I "heard" him but was not sure about the "obedience" part. I could not guarantee that for you or myself. Before long we reached a small village where there was a gas station, some low, narrow buildings, small shops, and a café with music booming out. In front of it were some old motorcycles.

"Let's get a haircut," Brahim suggested. "I know the barber well; he's a friend of mine. He smokes kif a lot but doesn't like hippy girls. Perhaps it's an erectile issue."

"What's bothering me now," I said, "is how to get to Casablanca."

"Don't worry," Brahim replied. "I'll take care of it."

He went ahead, and I followed him. I watched as he moved away, then stopped to talk to the gas station attendant. Then he walked off to the left, and I trailed behind him. When he reached an open dirt square, he suddenly stopped and froze. When he turned to look at me, I could see that he was stunned and bewildered. I guessed that something was wrong.

"Are you okay?" I asked as I approached. "What's the matter?"

"He isn't here."

"Who?" I asked.

"The barber."

"So what?" I asked after a moment's pause. "Isn't there another barber? In any case, we aren't murderers. You've made me so scared that I've been following you. I haven't killed anyone. If those hippy whores were killed, they themselves would know why. I couldn't kill a fly."

I started sweating. A weird feeling always comes over me whenever I do not agree with something I've willed myself to do. What has happened to me now, I asked myself. I started taking slow, deep breaths, a way that I have of protecting myself and preventing attacks of nerves. Sitting down on the ground, I surrendered myself to the internal world. Brahim came over.

"Teacher," he said, "we're only looking out for our own interests. We don't want people to be making fun of us."

"We're doing that now," I said.

"Don't be angry."

"What's my crime? They've found three hippy girls murdered in the woods or on the beach. But what's it all to do with me?"

"I've explained it all to you. Don't tell me we have to go back to Essaouira or Dyabat. If we do that, the shit will hit the fan for sure."

My entire internal world was on the boil like a cooking pot. Anyone who claims that the internal world controls the external one—shaping, framing, and changing it, and such things, is a liar. This kind of stuff, which Arabs tend to say, and French as well, has always puzzled me. But slow breathing, routine, regular, and continuous, can always put an end to such a state.

I watched as before my very eyes Brahim turned into an old black donkey, with a fox behind sniffing his tail; the donkey kept trying to kick the fox with its back hooves. But the fox kept moving back, cunning and self-confident.

I wiped my eyes with the back of my hand, then opened them wide. The only person in front of me was Brahim, still standing there in the square.

"Teacher," he said. "I've left a note with the gas station attendant. If there's a truck going to Casablanca, he'll get us a cheap ride. I've some money, so I can pay for you if you don't have any. What's important is for us to reach Casablanca and get far away from here. Keep away from problems before they get to you, that's what our ancestors told us. Anything they have to tell us is significant. You're a teacher, so you know that."

"You're the teacher! I don't know how I got involved with you."

"Don't tell me you want to get away from me."

"Go away from me now and deal with the truck and the gas station attendant."

He went off to the gas station, once again turning into a donkey. I saw an old woman whipping him; he had a heavy load of wood on his back. I could not help laughing at the whole scene. It would have been better if he had been a real donkey; at least then, he would not talk, nor would he know what his ancestors had said. Instead he would be carrying whatever was on his back, be it rocks or hay. I followed him to the station. When we arrived, I preferred to stay at a distance and sat on a rock near a low wall. I was not worried about what might happen and yet again surrendered to my internal world without any particular focus. It was a long film, involving angels, devils, tanks, and army officers strutting around in their uniforms. There were women as well, both bashful and blatantly naked. In the same film I saw men panting on top of women, drooling like so many dogs. The women disconnected from them, opened their thighs right away, and started screaming in pain, "Oh my God!" From the space between their thighs emerged tiny children like monkeys. The process between panting and delivery was rapid. The children started walking without even learning how to crawl. Then I watched them playing with guns and told myself they would undoubtedly fight wars against each other. I was convinced that wars start off as games. The film came to an end when I heard Brahim speaking to me.

"Let's go," he said. "The truck's here."

As I followed him, some of the images from the film were still dancing around inside my head. We got up onto the truck and sat between bags of wheat. Just then I had a thought: could Brahim have made the whole story up? How could I know? Could he have been involved in the murder? A host of questions now started bouncing around inside my head. The truck kept rocking along the road, and Brahim said nothing, as though he were feeling guilty for what he had done. Other suspicions dogged me: the eyes of the government never sleep.

"Do you two drink?" asked a man who was also lying down between the bags, clearly overcome by drink or exhaustion. "Look over there inside that bag of hay. There are two bottles of wine. Where are you two going?"

"Casablanca," I replied coldly.

"Oh, Casablanca's wonderful," the man said. "There you can live a sheltered life."

I reached for the bag of hay, and the man handed me a dirty cup. Meanwhile Brahim maintained his peculiar silence, like a guilty penitent.

"I wonder when I'll get home," I asked myself. "Then I can relax as long as we're far away from the town. Later I'll write a new story."

Afterword

READING MUHAMMAD ZAFZAF'S WORK is entertaining, and so is the process of translating it. From the very outset, his work made the headlines in that his writing was new, shocking, and in defiance of more traditional modes. Since those early days, Zafzaf's narrative repertoire has been both inviting and intriguing.

Muhammad Zafzaf (1945–July 13, 2001) was a Moroccan short story writer and novelist. He started publishing his short stories in Moroccan and Arab literary magazines, devoting his work to the portrayal of the daily lives of poor and ordinary Moroccans—alcohol, drugs, poverty, prostitution and women, as well as the hardship of the urban experience.

After Zafzaf moved to Casablanca where he worked as a teacher in a high school and later as a librarian in the same school, he continued to produce short stories and novels. He wrote a cornucopia of short stories and novels that were later gathered by the Moroccan ministry of culture in two collections—two volumes of his short stories and a two-volume set of his novels. Zafzaf's novels include *Al-Mar'ah wa-l-wardah* (The Woman and the Flower, 1972); *Arṣifah wa Judrān* (Curbs and Walls, 1974); *Afwāh wāsiʿah* (Wide-Open Mouths, 1976); *Qubūr fī al-māʾ* (Submarine Graveyard, 1978); *Al-Afʿā wa-al-Baḥr*

(The Snake and the Sea, 1979); *Bayḍat al-dīk* (The Rooster's Egg, 1984); *Muḥāwalat ʿAysh* (Trying to Live, 1985); and *al-Ḥayy al-Khalfī* (The Backward Neighborhood, 1992); Zafzaf's rich experience reflects the Beat Generation, a phenomenon that had contributed to the art of storytelling in Morocco ever since his narrative journey began in the sixties. A recent anthology of his short stories translated into English was published by Syracuse University Press in 2014.

Muhammad Zafzaf was very familiar with international literature, including works from the Russian, English, and Spanish literary traditions, and of course—bearing in mind the modern history of Morocco—the French. Several references to European literary traditions occur in this novel—Alphonse Daudet's *La Chèvre de monsieur Seguin* (*Mr. Seguin's Goat*); the poet, novelist, and playwright Jacques Audiberti (1899–1965); André Gide's *Si le grain ne meurt* (*If It Die . . .*); Salma Lagerlöf (1858–1909), the novelist and first female and Swedish author to win the Nobel Prize for Literature; and Albert Camus's *L'Étranger* (*The Stranger*). The last work is also referred to in an astute way when Zafzaf writes, "Once I could tell for certain that the knife she was holding did not belong to the 'stranger,' but was European, I started running crazily across the grass and through the trees till I got back to the town" (54), a reference to Camus's famous work that has recently been the subject of a reverse cultural interpretation in Kamel Daoud's *Meursault, contre-enquête* (*The Meurseault Investigation*, 2014).

Al-tha'lab alladhī yaẓhar wa-yakhtafī (*The Elusive Fox*, 1985) is a not just another novel by Muhammad Zafzaf. It is a portrait of a city, of personal experience and drifting. It is also an account of an historical period, one defined by rapidly shifting cultural, social, and political trends in Morocco. This novel also highlights Zafzaf's unique style, writing technique, and modes of expression. He was still a young man during the 1960s and is thus likely to have experienced and lived some of the situations and attitudes described in this work rather than merely observing them from a distance. The Moroccan critic Ahmad Bouzfour describes Muhammad Zafzaf's experience as "a cocktail of misery, sarcasm, and doubt . . . , of mendicancy, temptation and drunkenness,"[1] while Driss Khoury, another Moroccan writer, substantiates that opinion, adding that Zafzaf "never renounced the role of literature as being a self-reflexive process."[2] Khoury also notes that Zafzaf's mode of writing was based on his

1. Ahmad Bouzfour, "The Giving Tree" (in Arabic), Afaq ("Horizons"), *Union des Écrivains du Maroc* (Journal of the Moroccan Writers' Union), no. 61/62 (1999): 218.

2. Driss Khoury, "Muhammad Zafzaf, the Elusive Writer" (in Arabic), Afaq, ("Horizons"), *Union des Écrivains du Maroc* (Journal of the Moroccan Writers' Union), no. 61/62 (1999): 240.

awareness of things going on around him and on astute observation of both characters and places.[3]

I've chosen to bring this novel to the English reader in order to attest to the importance of Muhammad Zafzaf, express my deepest respect, and generate interest in Moroccan literature. I got to know Mr. Zafzaf personally when I was working on his short stories even though most of our conversations were over the phone. Our plan to meet in person in Casablanca was thwarted when he fell ill and was sent to hospital in France; he passed away before we had a chance to meet in person.

Undertaking the task of translating Zafzaf has been very challenging, especially the cultural aspect of his work. However, the significant contribution and assistance of Roger Allen has made the translation of this novel possible. I am deeply grateful to him for his assistance, encouragement, and collaboration on this and other works, such as a previous translation of short stories by Muḥammad Zafzaf, *Monarch of the Square: An Anthology of Muḥammad Zafzaf's Short Stories* (2014).

Mbarek Sryfi
Newtown, PA
May 2014

3. Ibid., 243.

Muhammad Zafzaf (1945–2001) was one of the most prominent writers of the Maghreb. The author of dozens of novels and short stories, Zafzaf was celebrated for his innovative, modernist, and aesthetic literature rooted in the detailed daily anxieties of the ordinary Moroccan.

Mbarek Sryfi is a lecturer at the University of Pennsylvania. His translations have appeared in *CELAAN*, *Metamorphoses*, *World Literature Today*, and *Banipal*. He has published with Roger Allen *Monarch of the Square: An Anthology of Muhammad Zafzaf's Short Stories* (Syracuse University Press, 2014) and with Eric Sellin Abdelfettah Kilito's *Arabs and the Art of Storytelling* (Syracuse University Press, 2014).

Roger Allen is Sascha Jane Patterson Harvie Professor of Social Thought and Comparative Ethics, School of Arts and Sciences, and professor emeritus of Arabic and comparative literature at the University of Pennsylvania.